THE GREEK'S OUTRAGEOUS MARRIAGE DEAL

RACHAEL THOMAS

Fabrian Books

Published in Great Britain in 2021 by:

Fabrian Books

Kent

England

www.fabrianbooks.com

Editing by

Joanne Grant

www.joannemgrant.com

Proofreading by

juliaproofreader.wordpress.com

Cover design by

www.bernistevenscoverdesign.com

Formatting by

authorhelp.uk

Print Book edition © January 2021

ISBN: 978-1-9993623-2-4

For Sonia Duggan of Inspirational Coaching who guided me through a difficult time in my life and Joanne Grant of Joanne Grant Writer's Coaching who helped me regain my belief in myself as a writer. I couldn't have written and published this book without either of you!

THE GREEK'S OUTRAGEOUS MARRIAGE DEAL

CHAPTER ONE

Kostas Kyriakou's thoughts were jumbled. Incoherent. He craved the buzz exertion would bring and dived into his infinity pool, relishing the cold shock to his body. Savagely he powered through the water, breaking the surface and swimming to the end. But it didn't do anything. All he could think of was his estranged wife. And her call, out of the blue yesterday, to meet.

He paused to look out over the Cretan Sea sparkling in the early morning sun, held ransom by thoughts of Athena, the woman he'd married almost a year ago.

With a growled profanity he turned and pushed off the side and up the length of the pool, his face beneath the water as he swam to the other end. But still questions about Athena persisted. Dragging his attention from everything else that was important. His charity's gala party this evening. His latest deal negotiations. Everything.

He stood in the waist-high water at the shallow end of the pool, unable to settle even to his morning ritual of swimming. What did Athena want? And why now? Those questions demanded answers. As did the many questions she'd left behind, when she'd walked out of their marriage, only two months after the wedding.

The woman he'd believed he'd spend the rest of his life with and the woman he'd thought had loved him, clearly hadn't. Damn it, she hadn't even given him – them – a chance.

So, what did Athena want? Again, the question reared up, like a wild stallion. And why now? He should have demanded more information when she'd phoned, but the thought of seeing her again, of a lunch date with Athena, had been too much to resist. She'd given away nothing. Not her reasons or her emotions.

He'd play it her way. For now.

Irritation drove him back into action and beneath the surface. His strokes long and powerful, moving his body fluidly through the water. With barely a pause for breath, he pushed off at the end and powered back down the length of his pool. It didn't assuage the anger or the irritation. Frustration drove him on, continuing the lengths until all he could hear was the roar of water in his ears.

He came to an abrupt halt at the end of the pool, his breathing hard and deep after such a ruthless pace. He rested his arms on the edge, looking out over the view of the sea as if it were going to yield the answers he sought.

The sensation of being watched slithered down his back, like a fish slipping away from a net. He stilled as he heard footsteps. Heels clipping softly on the terrace. Women's heels. Instantly he was on high alert. There was only one woman his staff would allow across the threshold of the sanctuary of his villa.

Athena.

Nonchalantly he turned in the water, spreading his arms out either side of him on the edge of the pool, as he looked towards the villa. Athena stood at the end of the pool, her slender body accentuated by the cropped white fitted jumper which showed off her very sexy midriff, and her short white skirt fluttering in the warm wind.

Inwardly he groaned as his body responded to the sight of those long shapely legs which had so erotically wrapped around his back as they'd made love at the side of this very pool in the heady first days of their marriage. She might well still have that potent effect on him, but he sure as hell wasn't going to allow her to know. Not yet at least.

'Athena.' He smiled at her, satisfied to see her shifting uncomfortably beneath his bold gaze, but wishing her eyes weren't hidden behind her sunglasses. 'I thought we had a lunch date.' The devilish need to taunt her surfaced. 'Or did you mean breakfast? In which case, you should have stayed over last night.'

The warm September wind playfully moved through her silky black hair, and the blush which coloured her cheeks was all too obvious. 'No, Kostas,' she said firmly, as if she were berating a wilful child. 'I did not mean breakfast.'

He smiled. Already he'd got to her. She might look more stunning than she'd ever done, but she was as easy to bait as she had always been. Once it had been merely for fun, a loving playful banter. Now it was born out of the need to let her know he wasn't a push-over. That he hadn't forgiven her...

Nine months ago she'd walked from this villa, turning

her back on their newly married status as well as the future of raising a family here in Crete. She'd tried and sentenced him before he was even aware of what he'd been accused of.

'I haven't eaten yet, so you might as well join me.' He didn't wait for her answer, but swam slowly towards her, the soft ripple of the water loud against the enthusiastic chirping of birds in the gardens beyond the pool.

He reached the side, placed his palms on the already sun-warmed slabs and hauled himself out of the water in one swift move. He could feel her scrutiny. It burned into his skin, hotter than the sun, scorching a trail from his shoulders down his back.

Again, his satisfied smile couldn't quite be supressed.

He ignored the towel he'd left on the sun lounger and walked towards her. His body was on full alert, acutely aware of her and he knew it would be unmistakable – if she dared to look.

Athena's body tensed as he approached her, his reflection glaring back at him from her large sunglasses. His brows twitched briefly upwards as he remembered her stubborn spirit. She wanted to step back from him, but that stubbornness wouldn't allow it. He smiled.

Slowly he moved a little closer. 'Breakfast, *agape mou?*'

'Breakfast is not what I came for.' The words snapped from her, her blush deepening.

He smiled, enjoying the sensation of being a cat, tossing a mouse just because it could. 'Then you should not have come to the villa at this hour on a Saturday. You know I swim every morning.'

'I wanted to talk in private, not in public over lunch.' She pressed her lips together as if she wanted to add more, and the need to feel her lips beneath his shocked him. 'But I see you're still as impossibly arrogant as ever.'

Kostas laughed, covering that shock. Maintaining his position of power. Keeping his guard high.

She shook her head in annoyance and turned in the direction of terrace, where breakfast for two was being laid by his ever-efficient staff. What did they think of the sudden and unexpected return of his wife? More to the point, what did he think?

'Hadn't you better get dry?' She spoke quickly. Flustered. By him? He damn well hoped so.

He laughed softly. 'You used to like to see my body wet,' he goaded, unable to help himself. 'You would lie there on the lounger and watch me swim, waiting for me to get out.'

'Not anymore,' she snapped, a little too quickly as her head dipped a little, her gaze going down over his chest. 'Put some clothes on.'

'Clothes?' he drawled, enjoying the sensation of her eyes on him even if he couldn't see precisely where she was looking because of those sunglasses.

'Yes, damn you. Clothes. How can I possibly talk to you when you are standing there virtually naked?' This time her head lowered a little more. Where exactly was she looking now? He remained proudly before her, every part of him aware of her. The desire just seeing her again unleashed, ripping through him, as electrifying as it was annoying.

'I only have that towel.' He gestured to the white towel abandoned on the sun lounger and then smiled. 'And our coffee is going cold.'

'Just get the towel,' she said, clearly in a huff. Was his

near nakedness disturbing her? Did her body respond to him as his did to her? He certainly hoped so. Because she distracted him, in a way that was far too powerful.

That at least hadn't changed. Hell, it had been the one part of their marriage that had worked.

Too late he'd discovered the poison which had turned her from him. The lies her brother had told her. Lies she'd believed and a marriage built on the foundations of passion, weakened, and began to crumble. He'd been as unwilling as she was to strengthen those foundations, wary of revealing who he really was. Before her brother's accusations had doused their passion, sure that his past was safely locked away, he'd begun to focus on their future. Telling Athena he was ready to be a father, ready to take the next step with her. Just weeks later, everything was in tatters.

He and Athena had gone from hot passion to icy silence in nothing more than a heartbeat. Something her brother had proudly taken full credit for. Alexio's jealousy and lies had caused the decay to seep into every part of the marriage.

There was more, of that he was sure. Such a drastic change couldn't be just Alexio's jealousy. There had to be another reason. Her brother's poison had unsettled Athena. He just hadn't discovered what it was yet. How could he when she'd refused to see him all these months? Avoided any contact whatsoever.

Until now.

Why couldn't he just grab the towel? Athena forced her gaze up from the firm, toned stomach of her husband

and up to his face, determined he wouldn't get the better of her. The truth of his words still burned on her cheeks as he stood in front of her, wet and almost naked, openly challenging her.

How on earth had she thought turning up at his villa first thing on a Saturday morning would be a good idea? She'd paced her hotel room, not wanting to wait until their lunch date, needing to get this done. More than that, she'd needed to be the one in control. The element of surprise had been her plan, but she hadn't anticipated being the one to be surprised. Proving that all these months trying to get over him had been futile.

'What happened to the woman I married, the woman who liked nothing more than to watch me swim?' Kostas's dark eyes sparked with annoying mischief and as hard as she tried not to allow it, Athena's pulse leapt and that coil of desire deep within her, that he'd always been able to set free, responded instantly.

'She walked out on you.' The words snapped before she'd had time to consider them. Inwardly she berated herself. She should have known he would torment her, push her to the very limit. It was how he lived. All he knew. Whatever he did, he did it to the max.

Heated images of being here, beside this pool with Kostas as he'd made love to her, taking her to extreme heights of pleasure rushed into her mind. She blushed again. That tight coil of desire unfurling a little bit more. She couldn't want him again. Not only had he betrayed her in the most terrible way, he'd reopened all the pain and fear of her childhood she'd thought neatly packed away. Pain she didn't ever want to explore, and his betrayal was the perfect place to hide that pain behind.

Yet her body still craved his touch, his kiss. She pressed her lips firmly together, closing her eyes, thankful for the barrier her sunglasses offered.

Kostas turned from her and walked slowly to the sun lounger, picking up the towel which had been tossed carelessly onto it. Despite all her intentions, she couldn't tear her eyes from him. His dark hair gleaming with wetness and slicked back making it look even shorter. His broad shoulders gleaming in the sun, his narrow hips and ...

She drew in a sharp breath. This had to stop.

'Something wrong?' he asked casually, drying his face, but there was no concealing the darkening of his eyes as he looked at her intently.

Stirrings of desire caught her off guard, whispering over her, mixing with a surreal sense of satisfaction. He wasn't immune to her and whilst it wasn't what she'd expected, what she'd planned, she fully intended to use this power she had over him to her advantage.

She would exploit it to get what she'd come here for.

She smiled and walked towards him, the sun beaming straight at her. The coyness she felt, the heated reaction to seeing him all but naked – and unashamedly aroused – should be all about acting, but it wasn't. It was alarmingly real. This man still had a powerful hold on her, but she had to remain completely in charge. 'Nothing that a good strong coffee can't fix.'

Kostas laughed. The sexy sound adding to the fire now burning deep inside her. Whatever was the matter with her? Just because she'd honoured her wedding vows and remained faithful to him, didn't mean he had, not when he'd broken them so easily and so soon after they'd married. She had to remember all Alexio had revealed about her husband. The woman he'd been caught in a compromising position with. She had to remember his betrayal had replaced their love.

Of course, that was it. She hadn't known any tenderness, any desire since she'd walked away from her marriage. Her body had simply gone into overdrive the minute she'd seen the man she'd once loved, the man she'd been unable to resist.

'Coffee it is, *agape mou.*' Kostas hung the far too small towel round his neck, his bronzed and damp body still alarmingly uncovered as he fixed her with one of those looks, raising his brows suggestively. 'After you.' He gestured her to lead the way to the bougainvillea-covered terrace.

Boldly she walked ahead of him, achingly aware that he was watching her every move. Each step she took intensified the heat from his gaze and the slow thrum of desire seeing him again had induced, became ever more potent. Even harder to ignore. But she would ignore it. Completely.

With poise she seated herself at the table as he pulled out her chair. It was the closest she'd got to him and his masculine scent, devoid of any cologne, invaded her senses. She looked up at him and instantly wished she hadn't. He was far too near, his head close enough that if she wanted to she could tilt her chin up and be kissed.

He'd done that many times in the early days of their marriage. A kiss that had promised so much more, but from a man who hadn't been able to keep that promise. Unable to help herself, she slicked her tongue over her lips, the movement snaring Kostas's attention. The darkness of his eyes becoming like a velvety midnight sky as the unmistakable swirl of desire filled them.

Heaven help her, she wanted him to kiss her. She wanted to taste his lips on hers again. To lose herself in the desire. In him.

'Thank you,' she said, slamming the brakes on that thought and turning her attention instead to the rich dark Greek coffee. His staff had remembered just how she liked it.

'Why are you here, Athena?' he asked as he sat down, pointedly ignoring his coffee. His dark eyes, now without a trace of humour or desire, bored into her. Had she imagined what she'd just seen in them? 'What is so important that you'd come here, now, instead of waiting until our arranged lunch date?'

Annoyance rushed through her, his tone almost mocking her. She'd been a fool to think she could just walk back into their marital home and ask for his help. But the reason for needing his help was the one thing she knew Kostas wouldn't ignore.

Her father.

'I am here for my father,' she said softly, a flurry of satisfaction slipping over her as he sat forward, a furrow of worry creasing his brows together. His eyes narrowed slightly.

'Is he unwell again?' Concern sounded in the brusque question and from the stiff alertness of his body, the quick flex of his biceps, she knew it was genuine.

She pulled off her sunglasses, needing to be able to look her husband in the eye. Carefully she placed them on the table, next to the coffee she suddenly no longer wanted, her hand lingering over them. Nervousness got the better of her briefly and she pressed her lips together. A childhood habit she'd never quite been able to shake off after losing her mother so young.

'He is,' she said on a sigh and looked at Kostas. He searched her face, as if wanting her to be telling him lies, but it was true. Her father's cancer had returned and this time, the prognosis wasn't as good. 'He's been in remission for so long I almost believed we'd never face this nightmare again, but ...'

Her words trailed off. She couldn't voice the reality.

Kostas reached out and placed his hand over hers. 'He has fighting spirit, Athena, you have to believe that. It saved him before and will do so again.'

The warmth of his touch instilled the confidence she needed to continue, to tell him what she'd come here to say. She nodded, remembering her father's demand as she'd stood beside his hospital bed. He didn't want her. He wanted his son-in-law. Kostas Kyriakou. The man he considered heir to the great Petrakis empire.

Her father was demanding the one thing she didn't know if it would be possible to give. But as always, she would do anything to make her father happy, make him believe in her.

'I made him a promise,' she said, sliding her hand out from beneath Kostas's, trying not to notice the flash of annoyance in his eyes.

'A promise?' The suspicion in his voice made her breath catch in her throat as she nodded at him. 'And this promise. Does it concern me? Us?'

Anger surged through her like hot molten lava. Kostas was like an adopted son to her father. He knew that. But with the tragic loss of her brother six months ago, that position in her father's eyes had been elevated, and he remained adamant Kostas would never risk the reputation or fortune of the family as Alexio had claimed. Kostas could do no wrong and her father wanted him back – at any price. And she was the one who would be paying that price in so many ways.

Even when Alexio had blurted out, anger making his voice icy, that Kostas had a mistress, her father had denied a man with the same values and beliefs as him was capable of such treachery.

She hadn't wanted to believe Alexio. But he was her brother. He'd been there for her all her life, especially when her father's grief made him shut her out after their mother's death. She trusted her brother. Loved him. And believed him.

'It does.' Those two words were firmer than she'd intended as she fought against Kostas's betrayal. Alexio's insistence that Kostas had only married her to further his business ambitions, that he was simply using her and her father, had played to her insecurities.

It had been safer to believe Alexio, easier than owning her fear. Especially when Kostas's talk of the future had forced her to face the reality that she couldn't ever be what he wanted her to be.

'And why would that be?' Kostas asked, determined not to make this easy for Athena. She'd walked out on him. Believed her lying and jealous brother. Why the hell should he make this easy for her? His pride had kept him from fighting for his marriage, from stopping her walking away. He'd thought she'd return within weeks, but the accident which had claimed her brother's life had torn them apart so far there had been no way back.

But now she was here. For her father.

Kostas knew what she wanted. And why. He knew Sebastianos was a proud, traditional man who would never accept the breakdown of their marriage.

It wasn't what he wanted either. Separation hadn't been part of his plans and divorce most certainly wasn't. Marriage had been as much about proving to himself he was better than his father as it was making a life with Athena. Kostas also held those traditional values and for the old man's sake, he'd revive their marriage. But Athena had to ask him.

He looked at Athena, as the warm breeze played with her long dark hair. His fingers itched to feel its softness, and he clenched them hard into fists.

'My father never got over our breakup. You are as much a son to him as Alexio was.' Athena looked at him, her caramel eyes pleading with him. She blinked rapidly and shook her head, her long blue earrings swaying wildly, catching his attention.

He sat back, all too aware that his state of near undress was making this even more difficult for her. Satisfaction sluiced over him, but he maintained his focus. 'Your brother didn't share his opinion.'

Her gaze flew to his. She took a deep breath, as if she was about to say something, then pressed her lips together and looked down. At least she'd thought better of defending her good-for-nothing brother.

She picked up her sunglasses from the table and slid them on top of her head. 'I'm not discussing Alexio with you now. The only thing that matters right now, and the reason I am here, is making my father happy.'

'And just how do you propose to do that?' He couldn't help himself. The mere thought of the damage that Alexio had done to his business filled him with such anger he could barely remain seated. Those bad deals he'd labelled Kostas's were one thing. But whatever it was he'd said to Athena, ending his marriage, was a step too far.

The pained expression on Athena's lovely face stabbed at his conscience. He shouldn't be making this so hard for her, but if she wanted him back – as her husband – she damn well had to ask him.

'By returning to Athens. With you.' Her chin lifted ever so slightly, and her shoulders moved back in a challenging gesture that pushed her pert breasts out. He ignored the stab of lust that fired through him and savagely pulled the towel from around his neck, dropping it over the hardening evidence of that lust. Now was the time for focus, for not falling prey to the power she still held over him.

'You wish me to visit your father?' He adopted an air of nonchalance he was far from feeling, but the need to make her feel even the smallest amount of the pain he'd gone through when she'd walked out on him, couldn't be quelled.

'Not quite,' she said, looking at him with confidence that oozed sexiness. Still he ignored all his body wanted.

'What do you mean, not quite?'

'I want you to come back to Athens with me – as my husband.' He could see the effort of that request as her eyes filled with tears, and for a moment he thought she might be about to cry. Then Athena gathered herself, so quickly he wondered if he'd imagined that vulnerability. 'I need my father to believe we are giving our marriage a second chance.'

Kostas raised his brows, fighting back the smile which threatened the air of indifference he'd adopted since sitting at the table with his so very sexy and desirable wife.

'You need your father to believe we are together again?' His words were slow and deliberate as the one thing he wanted suddenly seemed possible.

'Yes, damn you, I need him to think that. He's extremely ill. Maybe even ...' Her words trailed off and he felt like the devil reincarnate for making her so distressed, but he couldn't allow her to see his weakness. And wanting the wife who'd not trusted him, walking away without a backward glance, was one hell of a weakness.

Kostas inhaled deeply. 'You want to fake a reconciliation?'

Athena nodded, her gaze boldly holding his. Again, he fought down that smile of satisfaction once more.

'And how long do you intend to continue such a façade?'

She looked puzzled. Had she even considered this? Maybe Sebastianos was in much poorer health than he'd first thought. Kostas wanted to make the old man happy. Sebastianos had given him a chance when he'd arrived in Athens as a seventeen-year-old wanting to make something of himself. He'd been the only person to do that. Kostas owed him. Even so, if he did as Athena asked, he wanted something from the façade too – something from her.

'I don't know.' She looked unusually flustered. 'I just want Father to be happy. After losing Alexio, he's not the same man.'

Kostas bit back a retort. Alexio had caused so many problems but even so, the old man must mourn his son and heir. Kostas had salvaged his business reputation after Alexio's lies, but he couldn't forgive the damage done to his marriage. The fact that Athena had so easily walked out on him cut deep into his past, unearthing the conviction that he, an illegitimate man who had nothing, didn't deserve a woman like her. That and his pride had made fighting for her, and his deep-rooted need of a happy marriage with a woman he loved, impossible.

'I am more than aware of that,' he said, coldness slipping over him, chilling his skin as if the sun had gone behind a big black cloud. 'But why should I do this, Athena? You didn't even acknowledge my condolences when Alexio died?'

'Flowers? Do you really think flowers and a note were condolences?' Anger echoed around them, catching, and lingering in the deep red of the bougainvillea flowers surrounding them. 'My father expected you to come to Athens in person.'

'But would you have seen me if I had come to Athens?' Kostas paused as Athena looked down into her lap, having the good grace to at least look shamed. 'No, you wouldn't. Just as you wouldn't after you walked out on me.' Kostas watched as she continued to avert her gaze, annoying him more than he'd expected.

'Our marriage was over. *You* made sure of that,

Kostas.' Anger glittered in her eyes as she looked at him, and he realised that it didn't matter what she said about wanting him back in her life to make her father happy, she still believed whatever lies her brother had presented her with.

Kostas refused to be drawn. How could he defend himself without exposing the kind of man her brother had been? Just as she hadn't needed it when her brother died, she didn't need that truth now, not with her father so ill. If he returned to Athens with her, there would be time enough to find another way to prove he was not the man she believed him to be. As well as a chance to have the one thing only she could give him.

'You can't even deny it, can you?' Hurt filled her question and he wanted nothing more than to hold her, to tell her the truth. But how could he when it would hurt her even more? He couldn't say anything, not when Alexio was no longer here to defend himself, take her anger.

'No, I can't and for that I am sorry.' He sat forward, abandoning the indifference he'd been using as a shield since they'd sat at the table. He fought against the need to reassure her he could make things better if only she could allow him to.

'Will you come to Athens and see Father?' The hardness in her voice knocked that sympathy backwards. She knew he'd always felt indebted to her father and she was exploiting it to the full. Maybe the woman he'd fallen in love with and married wasn't as untarnished by the darkness which had filled her brother as he thought?

If she could use almost blackmail tactics to get what she wanted, then he too would ensure he got what he got exactly what wanted out of this unexpected reunion.

'Very well, I will come to Athens with you and see your father. But I have conditions you must agree to first.'

'What sort of conditions?' Athena asked, the softness of her caramel eyes hardening to glittering sparks.

Kostas thought of the plans he and his childhood friend, Elias, had had to build their empires when they'd arrived in Athens to seek their fortune. The vow they'd made just before that fateful night Elias had not come back to their small lodgings. The pain of finding his friend's battered and beaten body had been like a stab wound and it had intensified his determination to prove himself. To show the world he was a better man than the father who'd turned his back on him and his mother so long ago. Now Athena's rejection of him had made it burn like hunger in his belly.

Kostas was not his father. And he'd prove it.

He leaned closer, inhaling Athena's perfume, winding back the last nine months. 'I want a child. A legitimate heir.'

CHAPTER TWO

SHOCK STOLE Athena's voice as she looked at Kostas. She'd run out on him, destroyed their marriage. And he still wanted to have a baby with her? His demand was just as out of the blue as the day he'd told her he was ready to be a father. Then her carefully constructed façade of being career-driven had been tested to the full as he'd hit on her biggest fear. A fear that was painfully entwined with her most longed-for dream.

'You want a child?' She finally managed to croak out the words, her mind reeling with terms he had no right to dictate. She might have walked out on him, but he was the one who'd destroyed their marriage, destroyed her love and trust.

Had he taken a mistress because she'd hidden the truth so well behind her need to focus on her career and prove to her father she could hold her own in the family business? Had she unwittingly pushed him away?

'Yes, Athena. I want a child. My own flesh and blood to inherit all I've created.' The firmness of his voice warned her he wasn't going to be dissuaded easily. Anger simmered higher, threatening to boil over. Making her heart thump harder than ever.

'And you want me to have your baby?' Incredulity made the words stick in her throat.

'You are my wife, Athena, and I want a legitimate heir.' Kostas's eyes narrowed as he looked at her, as if he couldn't understand how she could ask such a question.

He doesn't know the true reason why you don't want a baby. The rational voice slipped slowly into her mind as she looked at his handsome face, into his eyes, now filled with determination. *He doesn't know how deep your fear goes, or where it's rooted.*

She couldn't agree to that demand, she just couldn't.

'I want my career over motherhood.' She forced the same determination into her voice, hoping it didn't quiver as she was inside.

'So you said, when I told you I was ready to be a father.' His voice was hard and firm, forcing her to remember that conversation.

'How can you expect me to agree now when you are not committed to me? We don't live as a married couple anymore.' Her panic rose higher as fear and secret need collided.

He drew in a sharp breath, refusing to be drawn, to justify his actions – or defend them. Anger surged through her, pushing her on to make her point, to defend her actions.

'I'm successful in my own right. I won an award for emerging architect and have taken Petrakis Enterprises to a global level, proving myself to my father. My designs have been used all over the world as well as for my own villa.'

Athena paused, forcing him to acknowledge her success since they'd last seen one another. 'I'm not going to jeopardise all that now to have a baby – just because you suddenly want to play happy families.'

Just as she hadn't the day Kostas had told her he wanted to go to the next step, to have a family, Athena couldn't admit to him that the very thought of carrying a child, of giving birth, terrified her. And she certainly wasn't going to now.

Just seeing a woman heavily pregnant made her cold with fear even though, deep down, she wanted to be a mother, wanted the happy family she'd known before her mother had died giving birth to her baby sister.

Losing her mother and baby sister had rooted that painful and irrational fear. Her father had laid the blame on the baby for her mother's death.

Then she'd overheard him talking to family members in the days after, words which still echoed in her mind all these years later. *If it had been a son, it would have been different. Daughters are not what a man wants.*

Since that night, she'd strived hard to prove she was worthy of his love, of being an equal to Alexio. As she'd grown up all she wanted to do was make him see her, not just as an unwanted daughter, but a woman who deserved a place in his business empire as well as his life. Such a woman wouldn't want children.

If her father's request to reunite with Kostas was any indication, he didn't view her as that at all. His old-fashioned values – about marriage, sons, and daughters – still stood. Ever since she and Kostas had married, he'd put pressure on her to have not just children, but sons to continue his business.

'Yet you expect me to drop everything and act as if we are reunited.' Kostas's firm words dragged her back from the precarious edge she was balanced on. Her father's views had convinced her she didn't have any value and she'd believed Kostas thought differently.

Now he'd confirmed he was anything but different.

She watched him as he sat back again in the chair, long and lean legs dusted with dark hair stretching out as if he really wanted to reach out to her. She almost laughed. Kostas wouldn't reach out to her. Not when he already let her walk away once.

'I hardly think a few weeks of your time to offer reassurance to my father, is in any way equal to demanding that I have your baby. It would tie us together forever.'

Just saying *baby* made her want to shiver with fear, and she closed her eyes as she tried to rein in that irrational terror before it erupted into something uncontrollable. Before it dragged out everything else, she was hiding behind it. She certainly didn't want to confide in Kostas now. But the door to her past was creeping open ever wider.

The sun seemed to dim, and she was ten years old again, watching her mother as she dealt with ever stronger contractions, doubling up over her bed, crying out in pain. Her father and her brother weren't home, and her mother was in such a panic she wouldn't allow Athena to leave. Athena had been torn between staying with her mother and getting help. She'd known deep down that getting help was the best thing, but every time she'd taken even one step towards the bedroom door her mother had cried out. All she'd been able to do was hope and pray as she held her mother's hand that her father would come back soon.

By the time her father had returned, her mother's contractions had become so fierce she'd screamed in terror with each one, sagging back to the floor as the pain left her. Athena had been crying hysterically and had been guided away by her ashen-faced brother. Alexio had been as scared as she was, no matter how much he pretended not to be. But he'd refused to ever speak of that night.

'Athena.' Kostas snapped her name out, dragging her back to the sunny poolside and the beauty of the flower-covered terrace. The sun hadn't dimmed at all, she realised. It was just the power of that memory. She held her hands tightly together, the pain of her mother's grip engrained into them, the memory bringing it alive once more. It was a night that had changed her forever. Shaped who she was now – a woman who dreamed of motherhood but was terrified by the thought of pregnancy and giving birth, as well as heartbreakingly aware of knowing the father she adored would never see her as anything other than just a daughter.

'Athena,' Kostas said again, this time more gently.

She blinked rapidly, bringing herself back from the past, but as ever the terror she'd felt that night as she'd watched her mother writhing in pain, the complete helplessness, both remained. Like a shadow lurking in the dark corners of her mind. A shadow she couldn't quite chase away.

'You can't expect me to be the mother of your baby.' She shook her head in disbelief, as if the action would stop the madness, halt her pain. 'Our marriage is all but over.'

Her heart was pounding as memories clung to her, like the thick fog of winter she'd experienced whilst studying in London.

'I am asking you, my wife, to have my baby. My legitimate baby.' His tone was cold, devoid of emotion. A shiver ran over her. Where had the man she'd fallen in love with gone? Or had that just been an act, and this was the real Kostas?

'How can you be so cold?' She glared at him, needing the anger to hide her hurt and confusion behind. 'You can't expect any woman to have a baby for that reason.'

'I don't want any woman to have my baby. I want the mother of my child to be my wife.' The determination in his eyes burned brightly.

'So, divorce me,' she challenged, anger finally getting the better of her, making each word as sharp as a knife. Divorce wasn't what she wanted. It wasn't what she believed in and it would probably finish her father. But with Kostas's cruel terms for seeing her father again, maybe it was the best option.

Kostas smiled lazily, remaining sitting back in his chair as if he were just chatting about the weather, or something completely unimportant. The fact that his tanned and muscled body was on display made the reality of what they were discussing even more absurd. Then he fixed her with a glacial stare. 'I will not ask you for a divorce – ever.'

'But I don't know why,' she said, recalling how he'd once spoken of his desire to marry the woman he could be with for the rest of his life. At the time, she'd just put it down to him trying to say the things he thought a woman he was about to marry, wanted to hear. After she'd walked away from the marital home, he'd never made any steps towards officially ending the marriage, proving his traditional values – and pride – were as strong as her father's. If she couldn't give him the baby he wanted and he wouldn't seek a divorce, where did that leave them?

'That's not important now. The fact is, we are very much still married. You want me to play the doting husband, to make your father believe his only daughter is once again happy and settled.' He paused, his dark gaze penetrating deep into her. What was she going to do? 'And in return, I want a legitimate heir.'

He sat still, his near nakedness distracting, making it difficult to think, to take any of this seriously. It was as if she'd fallen asleep on the flight to Crete and was having a bizarre and fanciful dream. One fuelled by her secret dream to experience again all the passion she and Kostas had shared.

'You could have any woman you want.' The truth of her words shocked her, his expression showing amusement at her remark. 'You could have a baby with any of the many women who seem to fall at your feet.'

The damning words of her brother made that image painfully vivid. And it hurt. She'd loved Kostas and because of that love, she hadn't been able to face any kind of conversation with him. Leaving had been hard, but the best option for both of them.

Now she was trapped. Her father's happiness and Kostas's terms firmly wedging her into a corner. If she played along, allowed Kostas to believe she was giving his demand serious suggestion, wouldn't it buy her time?

'Only my wife can give me the legitimate heir I want.' The harshness of his voice cut deep into her, breaking her heart all over again.

The craving for retaliation surged through her. She couldn't help herself and sat forward in her chair. 'But why is it so important for your heir to be legitimate? This is the twenty-first century, after all.' That last sentence was charged by her own predicament with her father.

He sat forward, bringing them closer together, and she fought the urge to move away. 'Why, Kostas?' she asked again, her voice softer than it had been since she'd first spoken to him as he'd stood in the pool.

'Like you, I've worked hard. Made something of myself. I want to pass all that on to my flesh and blood. Every man wants a legitimate heir. I also want more for my child than I had.' Kostas's voice became hard and determined, his words echoing her father's, cutting deep into the pain she'd locked away.

'What if we don't have a son?' The question tore from her dry throat.

'We try again.' He shrugged as if it didn't matter, giving no indication that he would value a daughter as much as a son. But his answer didn't tell her why a legitimate child was so important to him. He'd always kept his past locked away, giving her only the necessary bare facts. Nothing had changed between them. Kostas was only allowing her to see of him what he wanted her to.

But wasn't she guilty of doing the very same thing? Even now, as he'd all but demanded of her the one thing she feared and wanted all at same time, she continued to hide behind her career. Afraid to admit all that she wasn't enough for her father, that deep down he didn't want a daughter.

It was too much. She couldn't sit here, having this conversation like this. He might well be all but naked, but so very much of him was still concealed. She let out a big breath and stood up, walking away from the table, from Kostas. She needed space to think. To breathe.

'I can't agree to that, Kostas.' She walked further, towards the edge of the pool. She looked beyond it to the sea so blue it blended with the sky on the horizon, allowing the peace of the scene to soothe her jangled emotions.

'Can't or won't?' He growled the question out and she heard his chair scrape back, knew he was moving towards her, but she couldn't turn to look at him.

Panic began to take over. 'I can't, Kostas. I can't – won't have your baby. A baby isn't a bargaining tool.'

Her breath was heaving in and out rapidly and when he came to stand close behind her, panic rose a little higher.

'Neither is a sick father.'

Athena gasped and whirled round angrily to face him. Panic laced with that anger made her movement jerky and she let out a small cry as she became unbalanced at the edge of the pool. Before she realised what was happening, she was in Kostas's arms, pressed against his naked chest, inhaling the intoxicating scent of the man she'd once loved to distraction.

. . .

Kostas held Athena close. Her perfume invaded his senses, taking him back to the heady days of their courtship and honeymoon. It felt right holding her once more. He'd missed that. Missed the intimacy, the sensation of her body against his. Her breath was deep and rapid, her breasts pressed against his chest and the desire only she could evoke in him reared up once more, making every part of him want her.

She looked up at him, her lips parted, her eyes full of swirling need, matching the heated yearning racing around his body. He should let her go, should step back from her. But he couldn't. They had become locked in a bubble.

A place where nothing else but the two of them existed. No problems. No lies. No betrayal. Just them and the unmistakable attraction...

'Kostas,' she whispered. His pulse leapt. Desire exploded inside him, coursing through his body, like a volcano about to erupt.

He wanted to brush the softness of her hair from her face, to feel her delicate skin beneath his fingertips. But to do so would mean letting go of her. Something he wasn't ready to do yet. Not when it had been so long since he'd held her.

'Yes.' He could only growl the word as hot lust reached every part of his body. He clenched his jaw against the primal need to kiss those full lips. Kiss her until she cried out his name, begged him to do much more. Just as she had done many times during those first hot, passionate months of marriage. Until the poison her brother had injected into it, had leached through that passion, killing it forever. Or so he'd thought.

She bit her lower lip. 'I can't agree to that.' He forced his mind to focus, unsure what she was referring to. Reality crept back, but still he couldn't release her. Neither did she seem to want to be released. She remained unmoving in his embrace, looking up. But there was a profound sadness in her eyes.

Was her father that ill? Was he being unkind, cruel even, dictating such terms? He rebuffed that idea almost as quickly as it came. After all, his wife had been all too willing to believe his infidelity. To believe her brother. Kostas had hoped that given time she'd see her mistake, but then the tragic accident had taken her brother's life. Kostas hadn't been able to defend himself against the accusations whilst she grieved for Alexio, so had backed off, waiting until she came to him.

And now she had.

He refocused his mind, bringing it back to what they were talking about. 'I don't want you to stay in my life.' *Liar.* He paused, his inner voice so loud he wondered if he'd actually said the word. 'I simply want you to have my child.'

'But...' Her voice was still a sexy whisper. She was as affected by him as he was by her. The distress in her eyes gave him a fleeting hope that they could one day put all this behind them.

'It is still there between us, Athena. That powerful sexual chemistry.' He looked into her eyes and smiled gently, coaxing her round to his way of thinking. 'Creating a baby will be enjoyable – for both of us.'

She gasped and wriggled in his arms, moving her body against his, setting him on fire with hungry need. She pressed her palms to his chest, pushing her upper body away whilst her hips pressed against him. Against the hardness of his arousal for her.

He loosened his hold on her, allowing her to step back if she wanted. She didn't. She stopped moving and looked up at him, his desire mirrored in her eyes. She wanted him too.

As if she knew his thoughts, she began moving in his embrace again, pushing against him once more, unwittingly stoking the fire of heated lust higher as her movement heightened his need for her.

'If you don't want me to prove that claim right now, right here – like we did once before – then I suggest you stay still.' His voice was growly and deep with hungry need.

Athena became statuesque in Kostas's embrace. Her whole body on fire. Her breasts full and heavy, her nipples hard and excruciatingly aware of his naked chest brushing against them, her white top virtually no barrier at all. Every breath she took was deep and hard. Ragged. She glared up at the man she'd married believing he was hers forever. The man who had betrayed her – her love – in the worst possible way.

The man she still wanted almost as much as she needed him.

'You wouldn't dare.' Despite the bravado which filtered through her like a mountain stream over rocks, she knew her voice quivered slightly – and that he'd noticed.

Without a word, Kostas moved them both away from the edge of the pool, but that drew her even closer to him. The unmistakable hardness of his erection pressed against her, sending a pulse of need thudding through her, pooling between her legs forcing her to bite back a sigh of pleasure.

His dark eyes were locked to hers, mischief sparking in them. Damn him, he knew she would be able to feel him. That she would know he wanted her in the most primal way a man could want a woman. And how much it had always turned her on ...

Exasperation rushed through her. This wasn't what she'd come for.

'Do you want to test that theory?' The amusement in his voice only increased her irritation.

'That is just lust.' Her retort was quick and hard, but he continued to hold her close. She didn't move, despite herself, unable to pull away from him.

'It's a little more than that.' He laughed gently as he spoke, his arms sliding down her back, but keeping her close, making her excruciatingly aware of him. If someone had told her as she'd got up this morning that she'd be in Kostas's arms whilst he was almost naked, and within an hour of meeting him, she'd have laughed. No way. She wouldn't fall for his charm, his sex appeal again.

Yet here she was. Unable to meaningfully push against him and break his hold on her. A hold that was far more than his arms physically around her. A hold that deep down, she didn't want to break. But she must. She had to keep a cool head, and to do that she had to douse this unexpected fiery desire.

She forced herself to create distance between their bodies, whilst remaining within the confines of his embrace. 'It is not mutual, Kostas. It is simply lust. Your lust.'

He laughed again, but thankfully let her go. She stepped back from him, desperately trying to ignore the shock of the warm wind around her body after being so close against his. Steadfastly, she refused to look at any part of him other than his face. She didn't trust herself. Not when her body had responded so willingly to just being held in his arms.

'Are you sure about that, Athena?' he asked in that so very sexy tone of his as his gaze swept down over her, searing a sizzling trail over her skin as if he'd touched her.

'I'm very sure. And if you think lust is enough for me to fall back into your bed, then you are very much mistaken.'

Who was she kidding? Her body was on fire. Hot, throbbing need pulsed all through her. If he'd kissed her seconds ago, who knows what they'd be doing right now...

'Is that a challenge – again?' He laughed softly, his eyes filling not with amusement, but desire that she could feel even this far from him. She should step back more. Give herself more space, create more distance, but like a wild animal caught at night in the bright headlights of a car, all she could do was stand and look at him.

'It certainly sounds like it, *agape mou*.' The lazy, sexy drawl of his voice intensified that pulsing aching need in her body.

Anger sparked through her, harder and faster than it had since the moment she'd set eyes on him, swimming the length of his pool. Then she'd been annoyed at the way her breath had caught as she'd watched his strong strokes through the water. Just as she had done when they'd first moved to Crete after their wedding. Now it was his outrageous assurance that she wanted him.

'All I want is for you to return to Athens with me, have the decency to appease the man who, as you once told me, was the only man to give you a chance when you needed it.' Her voice spiked with anger and she pressed her lips together, cutting off any further pleas. She didn't want him to know just how much she needed him to do that. Just how desperate she was.

Kostas raised his brows sceptically and looked at her. Damn him, he was far too sexy, and worse than that, had a powerful effect on her – her body. *Because you haven't been touched by another man since he last caressed you.*

'I have agreed,' he said with firmness, putting her on edge. 'In principle that is, but what of my request?'

'Request?' She gasped the word out. 'That is more like a demand. Blackmail even.'

'I don't see it as blackmail. We are striking a deal – to get what we both want.' He paused, his coal-black eyes piercing her to the spot. 'And those are my terms.'

Athena inhaled deeply, uncomfortably aware of her heart pounding in her chest. If she declined his terms, she would have to return to her father alone. And she'd promised him Kostas would come to Athens. To him. She stifled a sudden sob.

He expected her to bring Kostas home. The son-in-law that was more like a son to him. And she'd promised him she would, even though it was admitting to herself that her father saw Kostas as his heir and her as nothing more than just a daughter. But what Kostas wanted in return was too much.

How could she agree to that condition? If she could make Kostas believe she would, just to get him to Athens, to see her father, she could explain it all to him then, once she'd kept her promise to her father.

She tried to reason with Kostas without alerting him to her plan. 'A term that will have far-reaching consequences – for both of us. And the child.'

'That is my condition.' He moved towards her, making her pulse leap wildly again. And just when she'd thought she'd got herself back under control. She needed to get away from him. Her body was reacting too readily to him.

Athena shook her head, unable to believe he could demand that of her, trying desperately to focus on that disbelief instead of the desire he was provoking inside her.

'But we'd have to stay together.' The words blustered from her as the confusion of her emotions got the better of her.

'While the child is young, yes.' The calmness of his voice doused the last embers of desire, bringing her back to earth with a hard thump. 'After which, you may leave.'

'I don't want to bring my child up like that, knowing I will one day tear its world apart.' Her heated words flew at Kostas and for a second, he looked stunned. But only for a second.

'The alternative is that you return to Athens alone.' His icy words froze the blood in her veins.

'If I do that, you will be turning your back on my father.' She used their connection, desperate to get him to at least see her father.

But if he did, then her father would believe that not

only would Kostas step into Alexio's place, but that they'd have children. The heirs both men craved. All the work she'd done since joining the company after university, the awards she'd won, would be worth nothing. She would be worth nothing. She would have lost her battle to prove herself.

She couldn't say anything else. The shock of realising she stood to lose either way, robbing her of the ability to speak.

Kostas took full advantage of her silence. 'Think about it, Athena. Go back to your hotel and consider the deal.'

He was sending her away?

'But ...' she began, then words failed her as he moved close enough to reach out and stroke his fingers over her cheek, just as he'd used to do. Only this time, she knew it was an empty gesture. Meant to derail her. Well she wasn't going to be derailed so easily. 'You really want to make a deal for an heir?'

Kostas dropped his hand, the hard glitter in his eyes impossible to ignore. He nodded.

There might still be desire between them muddying the waters, but one thing was clear, whatever choice she made now. She was going to have to fight for her father's approval as well her place in the business. Her opponent, the man she'd once loved. A man who continued to have a hold on her if the trembling of her body was anything to go by.

'I have a charity party to attend this evening in Chania. One Kyriakou Construction is proud to support. A formal black-tie affair.' He spoke casually, as if they hadn't just had a heavy conversation.

Party? What was he talking about? Athena's thoughts became jumbled as she scrambled to keep up with him.

He didn't give her time for that. 'I will be at your hotel at eight. If you accept my terms, we will attend the party as husband and wife. The first step in our fake reconciliation.'

'And if I don't?' Her breathless question hung in the air.

'Then we need not see one another ever again.'

CHAPTER THREE

ATHENA PICKED up the small black clutch bag that she'd purchased that afternoon along with a dress for the party, telling herself it was just in case she decided to go. Just in case she accepted Kostas's outrageous terms.

How could she not accept? If she didn't, her father would see Kostas's absence as her failure. She'd promised him Kostas would return to Athens. But if he did, she had to agree to have his baby. And that terrified her. As did the thought of not keeping her promise to her father. It was one she'd fulfil no matter what price she had to pay.

With a sigh, she looked in the mirror. It was past eight o'clock. She couldn't put off facing Kostas any longer. She was already later than arranged. She'd delayed and delayed, unable to go down to meet him, because doing so would be agreeing to his terms for their deal. Something she still wasn't sure she could do.

But walking away wasn't possible either.

She was well and truly stuck between one of the

jagged rocks of Crete's coastline and the hardness of the deal with man she'd once loved.

'It's now or never,' she told herself firmly, taking a deep breath she left the sanctuary of her room. She couldn't put this off any longer, not if she wanted to make her father happy. Delay wasn't a luxury she could afford to indulge in anymore. She and Kostas needed to return to Athens – together – as soon as possible.

Butterflies filled her stomach as she took the stairs down to the bar of the small boutique hotel she'd booked into that morning. That seemed a lifetime ago. But it was only hours. The butterflies took flight as she reached the turn in the stairs where she could see into the bar. To where Kostas sat, looking impatient. Waiting – for her.

As if he sensed her scrutiny, he stood up, his eyes locked on to her. He looked so handsome, so very sexy in a tuxedo which fitted every muscled contour of his body, and the fear faded that her dress might be a little too much. Just as they had done when they were married, they complemented one another perfectly. At least outwardly.

She paused on the last step, her hand on the cool marble banister. Swallowing hard, she pinned a smile to her lips, determined that he should never know just how much this was costing her. That dark penetrating gaze, which heaven help her she still found so sexy, held hers. It was time. Let the façade begin.

Kostas watched as she walked towards him, his gaze sweeping down the length of her velvet black gown, lingering briefly on her leg as each step showcased her left thigh through the long slit in the dress. She walked into the bar, sensing his attention now on the diamante-edged cut-out at her waist. A daring style for a fake reunion with her husband but dressing more demurely and avoiding a statement gown would alert him to the fact she wasn't completely committed to their deal. That she was looking for a way out.

'You look spectacular,' he said calmly, as if such a compliment were a normal thing to say. As if they hadn't spent nine months apart.

She put her head on one side, keeping the smile pinned to her lips. 'As do you.'

'A perfect image for portraying our reconciliation to the world.' He moved towards her and for a moment her breath caught in her throat as he took her hand, bringing it up to his lips. His eyes snared hers as he pressed his lips to her fingertips, and she fought the urge to gasp as that zap of something dangerous sparked in the air between them.

She took her hand back, aiming for total confidence. 'The world?'

'Were you not aware that this evening is a charity function? An auction for the Christofis Foundation, attended by the rich and famous, as well as anyone of any consequence – and of course, that means the world's press will be not far away. Evidence of our reconciliation will no doubt reach your father by tomorrow morning.' He paused, allowing the truth of his words to sink in. 'Long before we do.'

Athena inhaled deeply, finding it almost impossible to maintain that fixed smile. Already he'd turned the tables on her, put himself very much in the driving seat of this deal. Damn him, this was her deal. Annoyance flickered through her as he smiled at her, his expression letting her know he was more than pleased with himself.

'I hope you are not trying to tell me you will not come to Athens with me.' The fear that he was backing out of the deal surged through her, making her panic, but she kept her voice light. She would never let Kostas know just how unsure of him she was.

Kostas paused as a waiter brought a bottle of champagne in an ice bucket and two flutes, placing them on the bar next to them.

'Do you still think that little of me?' He frowned in mock consternation, but she knew her comment, her doubt, had hit a chord in him. She'd doubted him in the worst possible way. Taken her brother's word over his. Left him without even an explanation.

Anger sparked through her.

'Of course not,' she said quickly, lifting her chin a little and looking right into his dark eyes. Now was not the time to discuss what had happened between them, to allow her hurt and annoyance to surface. 'I am merely concerned that such publicity will make you feel a visit in person to my father – as my husband – will not be necessary.'

Kostas laughed gently, that same sexy laugh that had set her on edge this morning, unlocking sensations within her she really didn't need right now. Sensations she hadn't been able to rein in, let alone hide from again.

His eyes sparkled and a shimmer of something dangerous slipped down her spine, making her shiver. Judging by the satisfied smile playing on his lips, he knew exactly what kind of effect he was having on her.

'Tomorrow afternoon we will return to Athens.

Together.' He turned from her and pulled the bottle of champagne from the ice, looking back at her as he held it between them. 'And I think a celebratory drink is in order.'

'To celebrate what?' she said all too quickly, realising her mistake as that satisfied smile of his grew.

'Us.'

Athena watched as he picked up a flute and poured a glass of golden bubbles. She took it from him, the tension around them growing with every second as he poured himself a glass and placed the bottle back into the ice.

The darkness of his eyes was intense. Filled with something else now as he looked at her, raising his champagne between them. Something far more threatening to her than satisfied amusement – desire. 'To a marriage reunited.'

Athena blinked. It wasn't a marriage reunited. It was a deal for a temporary reconciliation. He'd all but demanded she have his baby and then told her she could leave once their child was older. The thought sickened her. In more ways than one, but she kept her cool, lifting her flute and chinking it against his. 'To our fake reconciliation deal.'

'Indeed.' His brows rose suggestively, and the darkness of his eyes sparked with golden fire. 'Our deal.'

She watched him, anger and fascination bubbling away inside her like the champagne. She should avert her gaze, not allow herself to fall victim to the power of the attraction still between them. But she couldn't.

Like a woman drowning, she watched as he sipped the champagne, unable to raise her glass to her lips as memories surfaced of how potent a kiss from him could be. When he kissed her, he left her skin tingling, as if he'd infused her with the bubbles now fizzing excitedly to the top of her champagne. He was the champagne to any other man she'd ever been kissed by.

He was also the most dangerous man to desire. A man for whom betrayal came all too easily, and if her father had been even remotely convinced by all her brother had claimed Kostas had done, he would never have demanded she bring him back to Athens and rekindle her marriage. He would have hated Kostas like she so desperately wanted to do.

She'd believed Alexio's account of Kostas with another woman because her brother had always had her back, always looked out for her. But now, with Kostas eager to return to Athens, she wasn't so sure.

Her father had championed Kostas all along and she wanted to make him happy, make him proud of her. The only way that would happen was to be the dutiful daughter and bring Kostas back into their lives. But once that happened, her father would look to her for the next generation. As would Kostas...

Kostas watched her as she finally lifted her glass to her lips. His eyes focused on her throat as she swallowed down the bubbly liquid, which for once seemed utterly tasteless. Was she really doing this? Putting on a show of a couple reunited just to please her father?

It was like walking back into the den of a lion so powerful that she knew she'd never be the same again.

She tried not to think about Kostas's demand but as the bubbles slipped down her throat, almost choking her, all she could hear, over and over, was her husband asking her for the one thing she was sure she could never give him. Playing over it, the threat of him taking everything from her.

Fear and panic gripped her, dragging at her insides, whilst outwardly she somehow managed to maintain a cool, indifferent composure. She blinked, trying to focus, aware that Kostas was again talking.

'And now we have officially accepted one another's terms, we have a party to attend.' Kostas smiled at her. A smile of victory. Gently he took her still almost full flute of champagne and placed it on the table next to his. 'If you are ready to show the world we are once more a couple, that is?'

'I'm ready,' she said firmly, telling herself she'd take this one step at a time. First the show of togetherness, then the return to Athens to see her father. Would that be when Kostas demanded his terms be met, request his payment for his time at her side, as her husband? No, she wouldn't think that far ahead. Instead she smiled brightly. 'Let the façade commence.'

Kostas knew that almost everyone at the auction had been aware of him arriving with Athena on his arm, despite the auction being well underway with a fantastic selection of prizes. His event's organiser, Yannis, had greeted him with only the slightest show of surprise on his face at being introduced to his estranged wife.

'How is the auction going?' he asked of the man who'd been in his employ for almost nine months. Beside him, he could feel Athena's confusion, and once again he forced himself to stifle a smile of satisfaction. He was already surprising her, but could he prove he wasn't the man she believed him to be?

'The larger prize donations are about to be auctioned, but so far, we've surpassed expectations.'

'Well done,' he nodded his approval, somewhat irritated that Athena's late arrival had forced him to miss the start, but toasting their deal was something he'd had to do. It enabled him to keep up the show of arrogance she'd accused him of. A way of strengthening his resistance to her. 'I'm ready to give my speech as soon as the final prize has been bid on.'

'You're giving a speech?' Athena asked as Yannis disappeared into the gathered guests.

He looked at her, seeing the confusion in her eyes, now far sexier than this morning with smoky eye make-up. *Come to bed eyes*, he thought as he smiled at her, unable to keep in the satisfaction that, once again, he was about to surprise his wife with a secret he'd kept, even from her.

'The Christofis Foundation is a charity for underprivileged youngsters in Crete that I started the day I sold my first building project when I was twenty-one. This auction is to celebrate ten years of the foundation and to thank its loyal supporters.' He pushed to the back of his mind the other reason for forming it, the friend in whose memory the foundation was created, focusing instead on the surprise on Athena's face.

'And I made you late.' She blushed as she spoke, looking up at him from slightly lowered lashes. It was all the distraction he needed, preventing him from slipping back into his past.

She was so sexy, standing there in that black figure-hugging gown, showing off her slender body and soft curves. Just as he had done this morning, he imagined what it would be like to kiss her again, to caress that body until he set it alight with desire. Because if there was one thing he had confirmed this morning as he'd held her in his arms, it was that the desire they'd once known still burned between them. It might be tightly bound up with hurt and anger, but it was still there, waiting to be set free.

She slid her fingers through her hair distractedly and he noticed the diamond earrings he'd bought her as a wedding gift sparkling back at him. For a moment, the fact that she still had them, wore them now, heartened him. Then reality cleared that thought. Of course, this was part of her façade, her act to make Sebastianos happy. And she'd brought them with her from Athens as a tool to manipulate, to ensure he did as she'd asked.

And that dress. She must have known tonight was important to him. A night when being seen with him would be as advantageous to her as it was to him. He pushed that thought aside. Doused the pain of her attempt to control him, their deal.

'I messaged Yannis to tell him I was unavoidably detained.' His voice was firmer than he'd intended, his mind wandering to thoughts of caressing her body. He needed such firmness to quell that need, and the evidence of her calculated plans only helped.

Athena looked back into the throng of guests, gathered around for the final prize to be auctioned, a holiday on a luxurious and secluded Greek Island. Kostas took the opportunity to study – admire – his wife more closely. The diamante-encrusted halter-neck and sexy cut-out pieces of her dress were her only other concession to sparkling gems aside from her earrings.

But what of her wedding ring?

'I'm sorry,' she said softly as she looked back at him, her right hand lifting once again to brush her hair softly back in the way she always did when she was on edge. The gold of her wedding ring shone back at him. The ring she'd worn on her left hand whilst they were engaged. During their wedding ceremony, he'd made her his wife, placing it on her right hand. Where she still wore it now.

But had it been there this morning?

Had she continued to wear his ring after walking out on him? The question gnawed at him. She either wanted to make a convincing show of being back together, that she was fully committed to the deal they'd struck this morning, or she'd never taken it off.

Annoyance filled him. He couldn't recall if she'd been wearing his ring when she'd come to him at his villa. He'd been too preoccupied with the way his body had reacted to seeing her, to having her close when he'd been wearing nothing but swimming trunks. He'd been unable to think of anything other than the way he'd immediately wanted her.

'It all adds to the story.' He leant towards her, whispering in her ear, her perfume invading his senses as he did so. That hot kick of lust stabbed into him once more. He drew away just enough to enable him to look down at her, into the softness of her eyes. His attention was drawn to the fullness of her lips and when her tongue slipped out to wet them, he nearly groaned out loud. He refocused his attention, dragging his mind back to the reality of the situation. 'And that is what you need, is it not?'

'It is precisely what I need,' she said, a spark of fire glowing in her eyes.

He opted for indifference, stepping away from her, away from the temptation to devour her with a kiss so deep that they would set the room alight like the fireworks that were planned for the end of the evening.

Applause drew him out of the spell he'd allowed to be weaved around him, reminding him of why they were even here and not in his bed, giving in to the simmering sexual chemistry which surrounded them. 'I need to give my speech.' He paused, then continued. 'And I'd like you at my side when I do.'

'Me? Why?' Her lovely eyes widened in surprise and from the rapid deep breaths she was taking, he knew she was as affected by the powerful chemistry between them as he was. But he had the strength to resist. And he would.

'You are my wife,' he said firmly, then lowered his voice again. 'And such a photo splashed across the papers will be exactly what your father wants to see.'

He could see the moment she battled within herself, trying to find a way out of publicly appearing beside him as his wife. But if she wanted a convincing reconciliation for her father's sake, this was the perfect opportunity.

'You're right,' she said, lifting her chin up and looking right at him. 'So, let's get it over and done with.'

He took her hand and led her towards the stage, where the final prize was being bid on. Her hand felt small in his as he waited to take to the stage and thank everyone for supporting his charity, with his wife at his side, along with the knowledge that he would one day have a child of his own. Elias Christofis, the friend who'd lost his fight for life in those dark days after they'd both arrived in Athens to seek their fortunes, would be suitably honoured. He would have kept their pact and honoured the vow he'd made to himself the night his friend had died.

Kostas led Athena into the middle of the stage and began his speech, thanking everyone on behalf of his wife and himself. As he spoke of the foundation, the work it did for underprivileged teenagers in Crete, he could feel Athena's eyes on him. The sensation so intense, that he couldn't help but look at her.

When he did, he could see the questions in her eyes, the confusion. He smiled at her. Where would they be now if Alexio hadn't filled her with such poison about him? Would they already have a child? Anger gripped Kostas for Alexio, the man who'd taken everything from him out of jealousy. He pushed it aside. Now was not the time.

'And now, to celebrate ten years of the Christofis Foundation I'd like to invite you all to join myself and my lovely wife, Athena, outside for a spectacular firework display over Chania's harbour.'

The applause for Kostas's speech had rippled through her as rapidly as the shock of being publicly addressed by him as his wife. Cameras flashed that she hadn't been aware of, because she'd been unable to take her eyes from him as he'd spoken, sealing the fate of the deal that only yesterday as she'd flown to Crete, had been just an idea in her mind.

An idea that hadn't quite gone to plan.

The night air was cool as she stepped outside. The inky dark waters of the sea moved gently in the darkness and the lights of towns further along the coast glowed yellow. Kostas took her hand in his as they stood, looking down towards the harbour.

'I never knew you were the founder of a charity,' she said as he turned to look at her, still holding her hand. 'In fact, there seems to be a lot I didn't know about you even though we were married.'

'Are married,' he said, lifting her right hand up and looking down at the gold wedding band she'd slid back onto her finger, even if it was only earlier this evening. His thumb caressed her finger, touching the ring. 'We might have lived apart for the last nine months, but we have been married for every day of that time, Athena.'

She refused to be drawn on their time apart. Now wasn't the time or the place to have a discussion about why she had walked out of their marital home here in Crete. 'Maybe if I had known more, seen more of who you really are ...'

Her words trailed off as he looked at her. The warmth of his hand, the softness of his caress was undoing all the determination she'd filled herself with to keep her distance from this man – physically and emotionally.

'Then maybe it is time to do just that.'

He drew her closer, using only the light hold on her hand, and despite everything she'd told herself, she willingly moved towards him. It was as if time had slipped back. To a time when they lived just for making love to one another.

They'd been so happy and there had been many romantic nights in restaurants overlooking this very harbour. He'd made her feel so special, so loved and she'd devoured every moment of her time with him.

'Maybe it is,' she heard herself say.

'Athena.' The husky whisper of her name uncoiled the desire he'd unleashed this morning when he'd pulled her close against him, beside the pool. Standing here now, the only part of him that touched her was his fingers on her hand, but she had the strange sensation that they were blending together, becoming one. Holding her close, pressing her body to his as he'd done this morning when he'd prevented her from tripping into the pool.

She bit down on her lower lip, butterflies hurtling around in her tummy as her heart slammed so hard against her ribcage, he must surely see her pulse throbbing at her neck.

He moved closer, his head bending towards her. She drew in a ragged breath. He was going to kiss her. And heaven help her, she wanted him to. She could almost taste his lips on hers, the memory of what his kiss felt like so clear now on her lips, it was as if he'd kissed her only yesterday.

'Kostas, I ...' she began in a croaky voice, her breathing so rapid, she could scarcely say anything.

Deep inside her, that coil of desire had unwound. It was red hot and seeking satisfaction. Every nerve in her body was on high alert, and still the only place he touched her was her hand. It was excruciating, exciting and unbearable all at the same time.

A loud succession of bangs and flashing coloured lights made her gasp and she jumped back from Kostas as if he were personally responsible, breaking the contact of his fingers on hers, shock making her blink rapidly. After all she'd promised herself, she'd almost thrown it all aside and given in to the desire – the lust – which hummed between them.

As if sensing her withdrawal, he looked towards the firework display, now fully underway. She moved to his side and watched his profile as he kept his attention firmly focused on the display. Her heart flipped over. This was the only man she had ever loved and despite his betrayal, she could feel herself relenting, feel her heart forgiving, but she had to remember what he'd told her this morning. He didn't want her in his life. He simply wanted her to be the mother of his child.

She shut down those thoughts, so painfully close to her situation with her father it cut her heart in two, but still she couldn't take her eyes off him.

As if sensing her watching, he turned to look at her. 'I will take you home now.'

She should be relieved. If she spent any more time with him tonight, she was in grave danger of letting him know that the love and desire for him she'd once had hadn't been destroyed, but that it was waiting for him to reawaken it.

She smiled, trying to bring a lightness to her words. Anything other than allow him to know just how affected by him she was. 'Home? I think you mean my hotel.'

'All your belongings are now in my villa,' he said, looking at her, sparks of challenge in his eyes that vied for supremacy with the fireworks hurtling up into the sky.

Other guests were gathered around them watching the fireworks. She couldn't respond, couldn't challenge his authority to do such a thing without drawing attention to herself. That would have to wait until they were back at his villa, where she would insist on having the guest suite.

'That is,' she paused as she fought for the right word beneath his scrutiny. 'Very efficient of you.'

He smiled, his brows flicking upwards suggestively – and sexily. 'I am glad you approve.'

'I will approve once we are in Athens and you have seen my father.'

'Which I will do tomorrow.' He faced her once more, a serious and stern expression on his face. 'And the first of the terms of our deal will be underway.'

CHAPTER FOUR

THE WARM BREEZE did little to soothe Athena as she stood on the terrace, looking out to the darkness of the sea. The night air was heavy with the scent of bougainvillea, but Kostas's presence was the more intoxicating. He stood beside her, his glass of brandy in hand, as if waiting for her to berate him for moving her belongings from the hotel to the villa. Well, she wasn't going to give him the satisfaction.

'That was a very shrewd move,' she said into the darkness, not yet able to look at him. Not after the way she'd very nearly betrayed herself as the firework display had got underway. A few seconds more and her lips would have met his...

'I am glad you see it that way.' His voice was firm but gentle and a skitter of awareness ran over her as those butterflies regrouped in her stomach. 'I knew there would be media interest in us, speculation about a reconciliation once we were seen together that wouldn't have been helped by us parting at the end of the evening. I made the arrangements whilst waiting for you at the hotel.'

That will teach you to be late.

She kept her gaze rigidly fixed on the darkness of the sea, moving softly beneath the starlight, the almost full moon hanging low in the velvet sky. A perfect night for lovers. But they were not lovers.

Once he would have stood behind her looking at the moon and kissed the back of her neck softly, until she had to close her eyes and give in to the desire. He'd turn her gently in his arms and kiss her deeply, making her heart race and her head spin. Every kiss more intoxicating than the last.

She blinked back the memory of what could never be again.

'I trust my belongings are now in the guest suite.' After that moment when she had almost kissed him, she needed to be in the guest suite. How could she want him so much when they hadn't addressed any of the problems which had made her walk away? She had to stamp out this desire, as if it were a fire taking hold in the dry grass of the hills. Her father was her priority. That and proving to him she was more than just his daughter. Not her body's wayward desires. And most certainly not lust.

Silence met her comment. It hung heavy in the warm night air, wrapping itself around them. Then the clink of ice against glass as Kostas took a swig of brandy. A drink she'd declined, not wanting to indulge in any more alcohol. The champagne she'd enjoyed at the charity function had clearly dulled her inhibitions.

Just being here, standing on the terrace in the soft light from the stars and the moon was reckless.

Dangerous to the woman she'd once been when she'd loved him with all her heart. The woman she hadn't quite banished if her performance and thoughts this evening were anything to go by.

When he didn't respond, she turned to him. 'I may still be your wife, Kostas, but I am not going to share your bed.' *Because I don't trust myself.*

He swigged back the last of his drink and placed the glass on the table, then stepped closer. 'Are you quite sure about that, *agape mou*?'

Athena tensed. His silky voice was sexy as he called her his love, taking her back to those heady days after they'd married. Days she could not think about anymore. 'Absolutely.' She threw the word at him, moving away to prove her point.

'If you are to keep you part of the deal, sharing my bed will become a necessity, will it not?' Hardness grated in the teasing note of his voice, striking fear into her.

She turned to look at him. 'Once my terms are met, we will discuss yours further.'

He was standing in the darkness of the terrace, his strong silhouette outlined by the light of the moon. The butterflies in her tummy flipped over and began to flutter. She and Kostas had stood here like this once before. Passion and desire thrumming in the air like the heady scent of flowers. That night had ended up with her in his arms, being carried to their room.

The memory of the hot passion surged through her, stoking up the insistent pulse of desire that being held pressed against him this morning had unleashed.

He laughed softly. Sexily. 'I do not think there is anything to discuss, Athena. We have already agreed on the terms, on what each of us wants from this...' He paused, his words penetrating the heaviness of the air around them. 'Fake reconciliation. You want me to act the doting and loving husband for your father's benefit and well-being and I want you to be the mother of my child.'

She pressed her lips together as he moved towards her, butterflies hurtling around her stomach like wildfire, adding to the intensity of the need she still couldn't stamp out.

'And in order to have my child...'

'I get it,' she snapped, not wanting him to say they would need to make love. If he said those words to her it would all seem too real. Too tempting.

He laughed again. 'But not tonight, *agape mou*. Tonight, I will be a gentleman. You can enjoy the sanctuary of the guest suite – alone.'

Panic lanced through her. What would happen once they'd reached Athens? Would he consider his part of the deal complete and insist she keep her part of the agreement? They would be living as man and wife in her villa. But what if he insisted on more? Or worse, what if she wanted more? It wasn't that she wasn't ready to be a mother yet, or that she feared pregnancy. It was the sexual tension crackling between them. She could so easily forget herself. Lose herself in his arms, his kisses...

Anger joined the spark coursing through her as she looked at Kostas. The problem was his terms. They proved he was no different to her father. That he thought of her as just his wife. The woman to give him a legitimate heir. How could she still want him when he made her feel like nothing?

Whatever it was, it had a powerful hold on her. One that was tightening with every second. And one she was finding harder to resist.

He moved towards her, increasing the tension, making her heart beat faster, taking her breath away. She wanted to stop it, but just being with him, just seeing him look at her like that...

'Tomorrow night,' he said softly, too softly. 'We will be in your villa and keep up the façade of reconciliation. We will live there as husband and wife, will we not, *agape mou?*'

'Do you really think we will share a bed, Kostas?' She couldn't keep the challenge from her voice. It was that or risk the craving to be in his bed once more. How could her body betray her like this?

Her husband was a skilful lover. Passionate and considerate. How she yearned for the utter and complete pleasure he could bring with a simple kiss, or gentle caress. The only man she had ever been fully intimate with and she still wanted that intimacy with him, despite his betrayal. How could she?

Because his betrayal is just the cover for your fear. She pushed that glimpse of the truth away, not wanting to analyse it.

'We will have to at some point.' Was he teasing her? Or was the hoarseness of his voice because he too was remembering just how intensely passionate their nights had always been? 'And you know how good that can be.'

'We will not be doing anything about your terms until my father is totally convinced that we are reunited.' She forced home her point, refusing to be baited by his reminder of just how good they'd once been. That was before.

His brows flicked up and a smile pulled at his sensual mouth, drawing her attention to his lips. Lips she wanted to feel on hers, possessing and demanding so much more than a kiss. 'Then I will do everything in my power to ensure that happens as soon as possible.'

Desperate to change the subject, Athena launched into a new conversation. 'I don't think you ever told me how and why the Christofis Foundation was formed.'

Kostas stilled. Did Athena know more of his past than he thought? His insecurities surfaced, like a monster from a deep lake. Was that why she'd been so willing to believe whatever treachery her brother had accused him of? Because she'd discovered just who he really was – and how totally unsuitable for a woman like her?

'It was formed in the memory of a friend,' he said a little more firmly than he'd intended, and Athena shot him a look of confusion as he battled his demons, fought to keep the man he'd once been, concealed.

Alexio must have found out how he'd thieved, but that had been just to stave off hunger. Or how he'd punched and kicked his way through every day with aggressive determination simply to exist. And if Alexio had shared those findings with Athena, it was little wonder she'd left so suddenly. What women in their right mind would want to be with a man like that?

'You did once mention Elias Christofis.' She frowned and he forced himself to focus on the here and now. 'What happened that made you want to set up a charity to help underprivileged children in Crete in his name?'

Athena kept her attention on him and as the moon slowly rose higher in the night sky behind her, he realised what she was doing. Talking about anything other than facing the fact that she wanted him to kiss her. Ignoring her desire to be taken to his bed as he'd done, from this very spot in the first days of their marriage.

Intense heat surged through him, waking his body to hers yet again. He pressed his back teeth down hard together, in a bid to stop his body responding to that memory, but it was no use. For the second time in less than twenty-four hours, he was standing on his terrace, hard and aroused by his wife.

'We come from different worlds, Athena.' He stayed in the shadows, stayed away from the temptation to take her in his arms and tell her that talking – about anything – wasn't what they should be doing after nine months apart. Not when such intense passion hummed in the air around them.

'I'm aware of that,' she said slowly, pausing briefly before adding with a certain amount of uncertainty in her voice. 'And I'm aware that you always considered me to be a spoilt little Daddy's girl.'

'My childhood, my family, was vastly different to yours,' he said, moving out of the shadows now he had gained some sort of control on his libido, thanks to the change in the conversation. But with his desire under control, he was more in danger of going back to those dark days as a young boy, when he'd stolen simply so that he and his mother could eat. Not that she'd really cared. All she'd wanted, craved, was her next drink. Something he hadn't wanted to get for her but had been helpless to avoid.

'And did Elias share your childhood?'

'We didn't know one another as young boys, but as young men. He'd been through almost identical things to me.' Kostas paused again, wondering how much to tell his wife, the woman he'd loved and had married believing she was the one. That she'd never judge him unfairly. That as Sebastianos's daughter, she would see him as her father did. He'd never counted on her being like Alexio, having the same prejudices as her brother.

'We also had the same hunger to make a success of our lives,' Kostas continued, not able to fight the pain that always swamped him when he thought of the way he'd lost his friend. 'We fought against just about everything and everyone to try and be a success.'

'And you are,' Athena said, moving towards him, reaching out and laying her hand on his shirt sleeve. The red of her nails was stark against his white shirt, and for a moment all he could do was look at her hand, recalling the blood on the floor beside Elias after he'd been beaten almost to death on the streets of Athens. He'd never forget finding him like that.

His eyes narrowed as he looked at her. She'd touched a raw nerve. Speared into all he'd strived to be since the first day he'd seen her all those years ago. 'Am I, Athena?'

'Of course you are,' she said firmly. 'Look at what you have now. The business empire you have created.'

His attention became fixed on the soft lusciousness of her lips as he watched her talk, stirring his desire once more. That was better than the pain of the past. The knowledge he'd let Elias down. Damn it, they should have been together that night.

'And *you* created it from nothing,' she said more softly, looking at him with sympathy in her eyes, filling her beautiful face. Sympathy he didn't want. Or deserve.

'Not entirely on my own.' The harshness of his tone didn't seem to shock her. As if she knew how unworthy of success he considered himself. But how could she when she knew so little of him?

Maybe that was the key to reconciling with her for real. To show her how he'd fought to become the man he was now. But that would mean letting her in, allowing her to know the brutal truth of who he'd been. If she knew that, he'd risk losing her altogether and right now she needed him – wanted him. And he wanted and needed that.

'Your father,' he began and saw those long lashes of hers blink rapidly several times. 'He was the only person who saw beyond the man who'd stood before him the very first day I met him.'

The only person who'd ever believed in him. He owed Sebastianos everything – including doing everything he could to make his daughter happy, as he'd promised he would the day he and Athena had married. He'd let him down, failed the one man who'd been there for him – like the father he'd never had. Damn his pride. It had prevented him from going after Athena. Because of that pride, a fake reconciliation and his barbaric terms were all he had right now.

. . .

Athena swallowed down the lump in her throat. This was the most open, the most honest she'd ever seen Kostas. But she sensed he was still concealing much more of himself than he was allowing her to see. She knew that act all too well. It was one she had perfected.

If they'd shared who they really were from the very beginning, would their marriage have failed? The question made her thoughtful.

'I saw that too,' she said softly, thinking back to the day she'd first set eyes on Kostas. She'd been fifteen, almost sixteen and he'd been like a god, walking into her life, capturing her totally. It was as if she'd known, on some subconscious level, that he was the man for her, the man she'd take as her husband.

Doubts slipped over her again. Had she been too hasty in listening to Alexio's claims of her husband's betrayal? Was it possible her idolised big brother had been jealous of Kostas, threatened by him even?

As Alexio had told her she'd been so hurt, she'd couldn't clear the image of Kostas with the woman her brother claimed was her husband's mistress. Not when she'd seen them together once before, the night of her name day party with when she was eighteen. A day when she'd hoped he would finally notice her and see her as more than the boss's daughter.

'I was only a teenager when we first met, but I saw you for who you were. A man hungry for success. A man I could relate to,' she said, wanting him to know just how long she'd held a torch for him, just how hurtful his betrayal of their marriage had been. And with a woman he'd once dated. 'Not that you noticed me. Not in any way other than the boss's daughter.'

Kostas looked at her, his dark eyes searching hers. 'Is that what you really think?'

The question took her by surprise. He'd derailed the conversation, taken away her opportunity of finding out so much more about him, just with one simple question. He'd made it all about her instead of him.

'Yes, it is.'

Kostas· sighed and shook his head firmly. 'You don't know me at all. Not then or now.'

'Of course I don't. We only lived together as man and wife for a short time.' Her thoughts and emotions were completely jumbled. Nothing made sense right now. 'But maybe learning more will help our cause and we should try to do that before we see my father.'

'You want to do that, now? Tonight?'

'We fly to Athens tomorrow.' She shrugged her shoulders nonchalantly, aware of his eyes falling on her bare skin and the tingle as if he'd touched her as he looked at her. That traitorous spark of desire was back.

'Tell me about the teenager who saw me for who I was.'

She smiled with satisfaction at his demand, his voice slow and sinfully sexy. As if he too felt the kick of lust stirring back up between them. As if he too wanted to know more. Not because of their deal, but because they'd once loved with such passion. Because there was unfinished business between them.

'When we first met, and you didn't even know I existed. I was fifteen – almost sixteen – you couldn't even look at me. But I had noticed you. Then at my name day celebrations, when I was eighteen.' She began, seeing his jaw clench hard together. Was he recalling the woman he'd been so much more interested in that day? 'I thought for a moment you knew I existed, because I certainly knew you did, but it wasn't so.'

Even now she couldn't tell him what Alexio had claimed about him and his past lover. Was that because he herself doubted it? Confusion muddled her mind, keeping the words from leaving her lips.

Kostas moved closer, so close she could easily step into the circle of his embrace, feel his arms around her – and kiss him. She looked up at him. His eyes were dark and unfathomable, but there was a softness, a sadness to them she'd never seen before.

'I noticed you, Athena. God help me, I noticed you that very first time we met. My boss's daughter. His fifteen-year-old daughter.' He looked at her, his eyes searching hers, and she desperately wanted him to continue, not to hold back as he'd always done in the past. 'And I thanked God you were so young. That fact alone put you out of my reach.'

She stared up at him, the feral growl of that last declaration still sounding in the softness of the scented night air. He'd noticed her. Not only noticed her but he had wanted her. That undeniable attraction she'd felt for him, that strong draw to him whenever she saw him, he'd felt it too. For her.

'Kostas,' she whispered his name. The same heady desire, the same unquestionable need for him she'd felt earlier in the evening, surged through her again.

It was wrong. She shouldn't allow it to, but she couldn't stop it.

Kostas reached up gently and stroked the backs of his fingers over her cheeks and even though she knew she shouldn't, that it was a mistake, she sighed softly, closing her eyes.

For what seemed like forever, his hand lingered on her cheek, the warmth of his fingers scalding her skin, setting a pulse of need thrumming through her like wildfire. She dragged in a ragged breath, not daring to open her eyes. Not daring to look up at him. If she saw even the smallest flicker of desire in his eyes, she'd be lost.

'Just as you are now.' The hard words jolted her back to earth with a slam and she opened her eyes as he withdrew his hand. He stepped back a pace.

Rejection stung through her as if thousands of bees had attacked every part of her body, every bit of exposed flesh. Worse still was the realisation that he was right. She'd allowed the attraction that still hummed between them, the desire that had licked through her when she'd seen him get out of the pool this morning, to get the better of her.

They weren't together in any other capacity than duty. Duty for each of them to her father.

Kostas couldn't believe he'd done that. Or the way Athena had reacted. If he gave in to what he wanted and kissed her now, she'd be in his arms and then in his bed. The powerful need he had for her came from so much more than nine months of abstinence from sex and it had almost drowned him. It was powerful. Pure passion. Once unleashed, it would be out of control.

'It would be too easy to give in to lust.' Athena's fierce words cut through the fog of desire which had him in its grip. He looked at the angry spark in her eyes and recalled all she'd claimed this morning.

Whatever had just happened, was it simply lust? The question rang through his mind, like the bell of the old white church which perched on the hilltop, overlooking his villa.

Maybe owning it as merely lust was the answer. At least until he'd kept his part of their deal and had seen her father. He knew instinctively it wouldn't be easy appeasing Sebastianos after allowing Athena to walk out on the marriage. He also knew that the old man more than shared his view on divorce and that he would ensure Athena – and Kostas – did everything in their power to mend the marriage.

So why did Athena think a fake reconciliation would be enough? Hell, the old man's health must be far worse than he knew.

'Then we won't,' he said as he moved away from her. 'It would be wise if you were to retire now to the guest suite.'

He needed space to cool his body, to remember just how much it had cut him to know she believed Alexio over him. Damn it, she hadn't even told him what he was charged with. She'd found him guilty without a trial.

He'd been so sure she'd be back once Alexio's deceit had been revealed. But her brother's death had prevented that, and he hadn't been able to seek Athena out afterwards, opting instead to give her time.

But she'd had time. Lots of time.

'Are you trying to banish me? Send me away like a scolded child?' Athena placed her hand on her hips, accentuating the sexy cut of the gown and stoking up again the throb of desire inside him.

If she didn't leave him now...

'I am respecting what you have already made clear.' The words snapped from him as he tried to control the way she was affecting him – his body. 'Besides, I have some paperwork to attend to before I leave for Athens.'

'At this time of night?' she asked, shock making her eyes widen.

'I wish to clear my diary and negate any need to return to Crete. At least until your father begins to return to health.'

Sadness washed over Athena's face. 'I am not sure if my father will ever return to full health.'

Kostas inhaled quickly and deeply. Sebastianos was the closest thing he'd ever had to a father. He was far more than just a father-in-law. That had been the final piece of the jigsaw. With or without Athena, he and Sebastianos would have enjoyed the connection they'd made instantly the day he'd arrived at the Petrakis headquarters, all but demanding a job. That action had been something which had earned him Sebastianos's respect and now guilt riddled him for not honouring that respect. He should have stayed in touch with the old man. But he hadn't wanted to jeopardise pushing Athena further away.

'What is the medical diagnosis?' he asked firmly, wishing he knew more himself.

'They have removed the tumour, but they are not hopeful that chemotherapy will work.' There was a tremor in her voice, and he clenched his hands into tight fists, not wanting to reach for her, draw her close and offer comfort. Right now, that comfort would almost certainly become something else. The one thing she had already told him she didn't want, even though her body was telling him exactly the opposite.

Kostas sighed, saddened by the news. 'Your father has plenty of fight, Athena. Be thankful for that, because he will need every bit of it and more if he is to fight this off.'

Athena lowered her head, unable to look at him, and his heart lurched, setting free that powerful need to protect her as he'd always done.

When she looked back at him, her eyes were full of unshed tears. 'That's why I want him to believe we have settled our differences. That we are back together.'

Athena's obvious heartbreak and distress made all his pain for the past pale into insignificance. She needed him to be strong. For her and Sebastianos. She didn't need to be questioned over why she'd believed Alexio's lies or pushed to keep her part of the bargain. Not right now, anyway.

Damn it, he was going soft. She'd come here to extract exactly this reaction from him.

'And he shall,' Kostas said firmly as he looked into her eyes. She blinked and one solitary tear escaped down her left cheek. He flexed his fingers, wanting to wipe it away, to offer more in the way of comfort. 'You have my word I will remain in Athens until he is convinced that we are reconciled, and on the road to recovery.'

'Then what?' Athena asked, fire filling her voice once more. 'You will want my part of the deal upheld.'

Kostas nodded. Enforcing his outrageous terms would keep him strong and his desire for her at bay. 'It is what we agreed.' He had to keep up the hardness, for his sanity's sake.

She lifted her chin a little higher, making her look so sexy he had to close his eyes briefly against the urge to press his lips to hers and kiss away that high-and-mighty spirit. But if what she'd just told him was anywhere near the truth, she would need every bit of spirit she could find.

'You really intend to force those terms on me?'

She was goading him, rising to his challenge, filling herself with fiery determination that would stand her in good stead over the coming days – if her father's health deteriorated. And he'd ensure he didn't dispel that strength. Instead he'd feed it, stoke it higher.

'You agreed to have my child, my heir. That is what I want from our deal and I fully intend to collect.'

With a huff of annoyance, Athena turned from him and marched towards the villa, the black of her gown, cut out at the waist and showcasing her back, filled him with raging need to go after her and kiss her into submission.

As if sensing him watching her she stopped and turned. 'I will see you tomorrow, when it is time to fly to Athens and not a moment before.'

He smiled, admiring his sexy and spirited wife. 'As you wish.'

'Oh, I very much wish,' she snapped and sashayed off, leaving him full of a desire he had no hope of satisfying tonight.

CHAPTER FIVE

Kostas watched as Athena talked to the doctors. If her concern last night hadn't made him realise just how serious Sebastianos's condition was, then being at the hospital, where the man who'd always been so full of strength and vitality was, definitely did.

As did the reality of what he'd agreed to.

Athena's voice, full of concern, continued to bombard the doctor with questions. He watched her as she shook her head in answer to a question from the doctor, her silky dark hair, now styled in tousled curls, gleamed beneath the bright lights of the hospital. The fitted white lace dress, which should have been demure, showed off her slender body, reminding him of what he'd turned his back on last night when she'd whispered his name. When she'd begged him with her eyes, her lips, her body, to kiss her – and more.

She turned to look at him, as if aware of his attention. She smiled hesitantly, then thanked the doctor and walked over to join him where he'd been surveying

Athens from the window of the exclusive private hospital, not wanting to intrude. He'd be asking his own questions later.

Her black heels slowly tapped across the floor as she came nearer, and any second now, he'd be able to inhale her sensuous perfume, which had wreaked havoc with his senses as they'd sat next to each other on the private plane he'd chartered. She smiled brightly at him and with her sunglasses perched on her head and her lips bright with lipstick, the confidence he'd always admired in her sparked in her eyes.

'The doctor is happy with his progress.' Athena lowered her head and smiled, looking up at him from beneath her lashes. 'He also said he has plenty of fight and spirit today.'

Kostas reached for her instinctively, wanting to offer comfort and support, but checked himself just in time. Instead he touched her bare arm, unprepared for the sensation of skin on skin contact. 'I told you,' he said as he fought to keep the control he'd spent all night instilling into himself.

She smiled brightly up at him, as if she'd forgotten to be annoyed with him. 'Thank you.'

He withdrew his hand, strangely unsure of himself. 'I'd like to see him.'

'The doctor said we mustn't tire or excite him,' she said gravely. Was she thinking the same thing as him? That just seeing Athena with her husband once more would do exactly that.

'Then I suggest we make this visit as short as possible,' Kostas said firmly, the sensation of being in control a welcome relief from the constant underlying need and desire just being close to Athena provoked. 'Just long enough to reassure him we are here – together.'

'This is the point of no return, Kostas.' Severity filled her voice, the lightness of moments ago vanished. The softness of her brown eyes was hard and focused as she searched his face, his eyes. 'Once we walk through this door together, we remain together – for Father's sake.'

This was everything he'd wanted since the moment Athena had left him. His wife back at his side and a future with his child in it. A chance to prove he was better than his waster of a father. The reason for their reunion and plans for parenthood, however, were not at all what he'd imagined.

He looked down into her beautiful face, his mind transported back to the day they'd married, to the ceremony that had bound them together – as man and wife – forever. She'd looked so beautiful, like a goddess with her dark hair against the white of her dress. Echoes of the woman she'd been that day looked back up at him.

'Kostas?' His name was a question, but her face was full of spirit and determination. On their wedding day she'd been young and innocent. Carefree. Then their future had looked bright and happy. But as the honeymoon had ended, and reality of life had invaded, they'd changed. Retreated from one another, hidden behind work, only coming together when the passion had risen to explosive heights. Sadly, passion alone hadn't been enough to hold the marriage together.

Had he unintentionally destroyed all that innocent joy they'd first known? Was he the one guilty of allowing the seeds of doubt Alexio had sown to flourish?

Anger zipped through him. Anger at Athena's

brother, the son of the man lying in the bed beyond the door. Alexio was responsible. He had set him up, but his untimely death in a car accident had forced Kostas to remain silent. Forced him to wait patiently for his wife to discover the truth.

Something she was yet to discover.

'Is this what you want to do?' Athena demanded, dragging his mind back to the moment they were now in. A pivotal and important moment in their marriage.

'This is what you want to do and why you came to me,' he said, looking intently into her eyes. 'It is what I agreed to do. My part in our deal.'

She swallowed, as if biting back a retort as he referred to the deal they'd struck. He hadn't wanted to be hard on her today, but if he was to keep control of himself, prevent the hum of desire becoming anything more, he needed to be merciless – on both of them.

'Yes,' she agreed, her chin lifting in that show of defiance he'd come to recognise as the new Athena since she'd arrived at his poolside yesterday morning. Shock rocketed through him. Less than forty-eight hours ago and yet it felt like Athena had been back in his life for so much longer.

'If I go in there with you,' Athena began again. 'It will undoubtedly excite him, but if you back out after that, it will most certainly upset him. Maybe even kill him.'

Kostas instinctively stood a little taller. His go-to stance in board meetings or when striking an important and lucrative deal. 'I gave you my word, Athena.' He hovered on the brink of saying more, of reminding her of the vows he'd made to her on their wedding day. Vows he'd kept. He slipped back from the brink. 'And I have never gone back on my word. Ever.'

He'd said enough. Shock slipped over her face, like a shadow created as the sun scudded behind a cloud, dimming the light in the room, and silencing him. Now was not the time to say any more. He'd made his point.

She reached out her hand to him, touching his hand lightly. 'In that case...' She paused when he didn't move, didn't take her hand. 'We go in together – as a couple in love.'

This wasn't the reunion he'd hoped for, but right now, it was the best opportunity for Athena to discover that she'd believed lies, that she'd walked out on their marriage because of her brother's jealousy.

Kostas took her hand in his, the warmth of hers infusing him with confidence that something far more could come of this fake reconciliation. He wanted to keep the vow he had made after Elias had died, to marry the right woman and father legitimate heirs. But he also wanted to be honourable. To be a husband and father who deserved respect – and love.

'As a married couple in love.' He lowered his voice, moving close to her, wanting to inhale her perfume – her. He wanted every part of the woman he'd fallen in love with to filter into him. He wanted to portray a convincing image of a marriage reunited, for himself as much as Sebastianos.

She smiled at him, conveying her gratitude without the need for words. But it wasn't her gratitude he wanted. From this unexpected reunion he wanted Athena to know the truth. That not only had he been faithful to her, but that he wasn't the one who'd made the bad business deals, losing all that money. He wanted her to see for herself how Alexio had framed him. This deal was the opportunity he'd bided his time waiting for and a chance to secure the next Kyriakou generation.

He bit back the words, the need to tell her what he wanted, as she turned from him and opened the door to her father's room, leading him in. Nothing could have prepared him for what he would see.

The man he'd admired was propped up in bed with a mountain of pillows, looking a former shadow of the man he'd been nine months ago. Anxiety and guilt coursed through Kostas. He'd never felt so apprehensive, so justifiably on trial. He owed this man everything and he'd stayed away, refused, because of his pride, to go after Athena. Sebastianos looked at him, dark eyes fixing to his and he knew he was far from forgiven.

'The errant husband returns.' The gravelly voice had more strength in it than the frail body in the bed.

Athena gasped and Kostas felt her hand pulling from his. He held it tighter.

Athena looked at Kostas as he refused to let her hand go and with her father watching far too intently, she had no choice but to keep her hand in her husband's.

'Kostas has come to see you, Father, because I asked him to.' She moved instinctively closer to her husband as her father, always shrewd, narrowed his eyes in suspicion. She hadn't bargained on him being well enough to argue, to stir up trouble.

She should be glad her father was well enough to berate Kostas – and her. But right now, her hand pinned in Kostas's, her body close against him, she was distinctly on edge.

'It is true,' Kostas said as he moved closer to her father's bed, giving her no option but to go with him as he resolutely refused to let her hand go. 'Athena came to Crete on Saturday.'

Her father laughed. A rough raspy sound, but amusement didn't reach his eyes. Anger his weakened body belied, glittered in them. 'And you expect me to believe that? After nearly a year of silence, of nothing, you expect me to believe that you, of all men, came to my sickbed because your wife asked you to?'

Athena's thoughts scrabbled. They weren't meant to be upsetting him, but he was more distressed, angrier than she'd seen him in a long time. The last time he'd looked so wild had been the day the news of Alexio's accident and instant death had reached them.

A day she'd never forget. She'd been at home with her father, nursing her breaking heart, desperately trying to keep her focus on Alexio's revelations about Kostas. In one fell swoop she'd lost Alexio and Kostas.

At the very same time, her father had flatly refused to talk about the allegations Alexio had levelled at Kostas. Each time she'd tried, she'd been met with the same cold denial. Her father simply didn't believe it. Didn't want to.

She'd assumed it was because he'd put all his faith in Kostas, had given him so much authority within the business before he'd gone his own way. Then the last time she'd been to the hospital, her father had told her what he wanted. She'd seen the truth of that request in her father's eyes. Now that Alexio was gone, he viewed Kostas as his son. His heir.

'I came for you, Sebastianos,' Kostas said as he let her hand go, moving closer to her father until he was looking down at him. Her father looked angrily back up and she had the distinct impression that her presence had been forgotten. Something she was used to but tired of fighting against. 'To see the man who is like a father to me.'

Athena knew her father had helped Kostas with his business in the beginning but had little idea of what he'd done or when. Things like that weren't discussed by her father, at least not with her. She watched Kostas, studied his profile. Saw his jaw clench as he stood looking at her father and for the first time ever, she felt she was seeing the real Kostas. The Kostas he'd always taken such pains to keep from her.

'More likely because of a deal,' growled her father then he turned his attention to her. 'You told me you'd bring Kostas back...' He paused and looked at her. Athena felt the colour flood to her cheeks. She must have guilt written all over her face. 'So, I am assuming you have come to an arrangement. Made a deal.'

Athena felt like a child again. She loved her father dearly. He and Alexio were all she'd had after her mother had died. Her father had been there for her, even though emotionally distanced by his grief. Even when he'd made her feel like a pampered princess, or Daddy's little angel, he'd never been able to soften completely. In his eyes, she was *just* his daughter. A daughter he didn't want or need.

'We did strike a deal,' Kostas said firmly.

Athena's attention flew back to Kostas, his words echoing around the sterile environment of the room. Why had he said that?

Her father looked from Kostas to her, suspicion blazing in his eyes. If anything, the exchange invigorated him. Even so, Athena worried it was too much.

'We can talk about this another time,' she said into the tension which had crept into the room, swirling like a dark shadow. 'When you are stronger.'

'What deal?' her father demanded, looking at Kostas who stood rigid and tall before her father's scrutiny. 'What terms?'

Inwardly Athena groaned. The two men who meant the most to her were as stubborn as one another. Neither saw beyond her, to what she could be, what she was. But even that didn't stop her feelings – for either of them.

She drew in a breath as the truth of that thought sank in. Kostas still meant something to her. He was still important to her. Her heart raced and reality dawned. She meant nothing to him. He'd already declared her surplus to requirements once she gave him the one thing, he wanted most. A child.

And what if the child was a girl? His answer to that question had terrified her. Still did.

'To make our marriage work,' Kostas said into the silence, dragging her from that heart-stopping question. He turned to look at her.

Warning flashed in his eyes as they met hers. She could feel her breathing becoming harder, deeper. He raised his brows suggestively and the butterflies she'd had yesterday returned with a vengeance.

He walked to her, but instead of taking her hand as she had done to him, he put his arm around her shoulder, drawing her close against his side. Her bare arm sizzled with the contact, his shirt no barrier to the heat.

Nerves got the better of her and she bit her lower lip. Her father's attention flew to that gesture. He knew it meant she was uncomfortable, on edge. She forced a smile to her lips.

'We are, Father,' she said firmly, trying to force her uncooperative lips into a smile of confidence. 'As of yesterday, we are reconciled.'

Her father shifted awkwardly in his bed and reached for a newspaper on the cabinet next to him. She watched as he unfolded it and opened the pages, then laid it on his lap upside down. The photograph that had been taken by the press as Kostas had given his speech as the charity auction took up half the page. But it was the photo beneath that caught her off-guard. The one she'd had no idea had been taken whilst they watched the fireworks.

She couldn't help herself. She stepped forward to take a closer look, feeling Kostas move with her. He looked over her shoulder, his breath warm against her neck, and she forced her focus to remain on the photograph, hardly able to believe what she saw.

Two people so completely consumed by the other, they'd had no knowledge that anyone had taken it. There was passion, desire, and sexual tension in the way they looked at one another.

A far cry from the two people who stood at her father's bedside now.

If she didn't know any better, she'd say the couple in the photograph had gone home that night and filled the hours of darkness with intensely passionate sex. But she did know better. She knew that night, unable to trust herself, she'd lie alone in a bed she'd never slept in before.

'This couple can't keep their hands off one another.' Her father's declaration shocked her, and she blinked it back as she stood straight, colliding with Kostas as she did so.

'What are you saying, Father?' she asked far more calmly than she felt.

'That I don't believe you.' He waved his hand in their direction. 'Where is this fire now? This passion? You can't mend a marriage with the icy coldness you two have brought into the room.'

'I was being respectful to you,' Kostas said as he looked at her father. 'But rest assured, we will be living as man and wife from now on.'

Her father's eyes narrowed as he looked at Kostas, and Athena realised how much she'd damaged the relationship between them when she'd walked out on Kostas. On her marriage. Because of her fears, her past, she'd rejected Kostas. Using Alexio's allegations to avoid a much bigger issue. It was time to finally admit that, even if only to herself.

'It is true, Father,' she said softly, moving closer to Kostas, slipping her arm around him, sending those butterflies into a frenzy. There was one thing she could say that might convince her father this was real. He would be expecting their reunion to produce children.

For a second, she considered the wisdom of it, but her father had no idea how that last night with her mother had affected her. How it had made her who she was now.

Maybe if she'd told someone her fears, they wouldn't have wrecked her marriage. But that was just another layer of smoke. Something else, however real, for her to hide behind. And far safer than exposing her emotions – her heart – to anyone.

Athena took a breath. She could feel Kostas looking at her, as if he sensed she was about to say something drastic. 'We want to start a family of our own.'

If the tension in the starkness of the hospital room had been high before, it now went off the scale. Her father looked at her. Speechless. Not something he was very often, and she could feel Kostas's intense scrutiny, but she didn't dare look at him.

Not yet. Not until she'd got her head around what she'd just said.

'Good,' her father said gruffly. 'Another generation to continue what I started. It's about time.'

Athena felt the cool dread slip over her, along with the icy fear that the thought of pregnancy brought. She hadn't intended to say it. Hadn't intended to give Kostas the power in their deal. Now, because she'd desperately wanted to placate her father, convince him she and Kostas were back together, she'd promised him something she had no idea if she could ever give him.

She'd wedged herself deeper between them. There could only be one loser now. Herself.

'Not straight away,' she stumbled over the words, trying to back track on what she'd said. 'But in the future. Soon.'

'Now I have something to fight for,' her father said, looking at Kostas. 'A man needs a reason to fight, don't you think, Kostas?'

Athena frowned. What did that mean?

Kostas pulled her closer, his fingers gripping into her arm, scorching her bare skin. She bit down hard into her lower lip and looked at her father as he glared up at Kostas, challenge clear in his eyes. She had to get out of here. For her sake as well as her father's.

'We should go now,' she said as firmly as she could. Her father's penetrating gaze didn't waver from Kostas. She should be pleased he'd become more of the man he'd once been, but alarm bells were ringing wildly in her mind. 'We will come again soon.'

'Friday is your cousin's name day party.' Finally, her father looked at her, but the relief was short-lived as the full force of his anger, his challenge, rained down on her. 'I expect you to go – together – and represent me.'

'And we will,' Athena said calmly, hoping to appease him further, soothe his anger. 'And I will visit you each day.'

'There are things which need your attention from the office.' He rebuffed her and looked again at Kostas. The fact that he'd allowed her to take over some of his duties at the office only gave weight to how ill he'd become. 'And yours. I want you back in the business, Kostas.'

'You don't have to do this now,' Athena urged her father, holding back the hurt.

'I do.' He glared up at her. 'But right now, I need some peace and quiet.'

They had been dismissed. Athena felt her shoulders sag slightly and realised how tensely she'd been holding herself. 'If that is what you want,' she said calmly, reaching out to touch her father's hand where it lay on the bed.

Her touch shocked him, but he quickly recovered. 'It is. Just as I wish to see the two of you together.'

She smiled. 'We are, Father.'

As if to confirm what she'd said, Kostas placed his hand on her back as she bent towards her father. Heat seared through her dress, and a small gasp slipped from her.

Her father's eyes narrowed slightly. 'I want to see you two together because you want to be, because you can't help it...' His voice trailed off briefly but surged back ever stronger. 'Not because of a damn deal.'

Athena swallowed. Could she give her father that? With Kostas's terms hanging over her – and her own stupid admission of starting a family. Inside she wanted to cry. She'd expected Kostas to visit her father and make it all better, make him better. Instead everything was worse.

'We should go now, Athena,' Kostas said softly and she became aware of his hand gently rubbing her back. Affectionately. She was almost fooled but it was merely a show for her father. Already Kostas was rising to the challenge. Making their reconciliation appear real.

She leant further forwards and kissed her father lightly on his cheek, the movement thankfully breaking the contact, taking her away from Kostas's touch. 'I will see you soon, Father.' Her voice was almost a whisper as emotion and the sensation of failure surged through her. 'And let you know the news from the office.'

Without another word, or without waiting for Kostas, she stood tall and turned to leave the room. Her heels clipped out a loud rhythm as she hastily made her way to the door. She needed to get out of the room. Out of the hospital. Everything she'd held in check since seeing Kostas swimming in the pool was surging forwards, demanding her thoughts, her attention.

. . .

Kostas turned to go after Athena. He was sure this hadn't gone as she'd intended, but her mention of starting a family had satisfied him that she was taking his terms of their deal seriously. That she would follow through and fulfil her side of the deal – one day. What was it she'd said to her father? In the future – soon.

'Go after her, damn it.' Sebastianos's voice cut through the air and he realised he'd been lost in thought, something he rarely did in front of others. Such indulgence in silent thought showed weakness. 'Go and make it right, Kostas. For Athena – and for me. You owe me that.'

There it was. Sebastianos had demanded his payback for all the help he'd given Kostas all those years ago. He wanted him to make the marriage right. To make it work.

'That is exactly what I intend to do,' he said as he stood tall in front of the man he owed everything to. 'You have my word.'

'Then go.' Sebastianos growled the command and flopped back against the pillows, spent from the effort of ruling his family, getting what he wanted.

Kostas turned and left the old man. The corridor was empty and for a moment he wondered if Athena had left him. If her deal was too much for her to keep. But it was a deal she wanted, for her father, and this visit had proved she would do anything for him.

He drew in a deep breath and marched along the cold, clinical corridor and made his way outside. Athena was standing beneath the shade of a tree, her arms folded about her body as if she were trying to offer herself comfort. The white lace dress, with the narrow black belt at her waist which had made her look so sexy before, now made her look vulnerable. And innocent.

His heart thudded and everything he'd ever felt then smothered for his wife when she'd left him, rushed back, threatening to take over. He wanted to take her in his arms, soothe her pain, kiss away her fears and tell her they'd make it right, that he'd be anything she needed him to be. Because of the attraction, the passion which still sparked between them. That was the key to making this deal work.

She whirled round and faced him. 'You've made everything worse. I should have known I couldn't trust you.'

They were here again. Just as they had been nine months ago. She didn't trust him. She believed her scoundrel of a brother instead of the man she'd married. And if he wasn't mistaken, Sebastianos knew that and had challenged him to make it right.

It wasn't what he'd come here for. He'd come because her deal offered him the way of keeping his vow, his need to be a father, to raise his child, his heir, without the need for the divorce he was so against. As far as he was concerned, divorce was failure. Just as the inability to marry the mother of his child had been for his father. Both were failures. But now he could be a father and remain Athena's husband. Their deal meant he could do that without having to engage his emotions. Without having to feel the love he'd banished to the coldest part of his heart when she'd rejected him.

'But you have never trusted me, have you, Athena?' He couldn't hold it back any longer. 'I will make every effort, do everything necessary to give Sebastianos what he craves, but I can't unless you trust me.'

She glared angrily at him and he knew that anyone passing would hear their conversation, but it had to be had – and now.

'How can I trust you when you made all those bad deals, nearly destroying the business?'

'But there's more, isn't there? Why don't you just tell me?' He didn't want to dance around a fire that was more smoke than flame any longer.

'Because you had an affair.'

'How can you believe that of me, Athena?' The sun was strong and glaring down at him, forcing him to narrow his eyes against it, but he didn't want to put on his sunglasses now. He didn't want to shield his eyes from her. He wanted her to see his innocence. His complete lack of guilt.

She glared accusingly at him. 'Alexio told me.'

He moved closer to her and she hugged her body even tighter, as if desperate to keep herself locked away.

'Do you always believe what you're told?' His cool words allowed control to chase away any hint of affection that had surfaced as he'd seen her standing so alone outside the hospital.

She blinked a few times but stuck to her argument. 'Alexio is my brother. Who do you think I would believe? The man I've always looked up to, the man who's been my rock for so many years, or the man I stupidly thought was in love with me.'

Kostas pressed his lips together and inhaled deeply, forcing calmness into his body. Anger wouldn't achieve anything. It wouldn't help to bring them together, to make them look like lovers. Neither would it help him convince her of his innocence. It had only ever been Athena he'd wanted. From the very first day he'd seen her.

He fought to remain silent, to take her wrath, but his pride wouldn't allow him to be tried like this and not defend himself.

'You should have believed the man who had loved you – me. Your husband.'

'Why?' Her arms unfolded and her palms stretched out to him in a gesture of frustration.

'Because it's not true.' Kostas watched Athena, icy cold disapproval radiating from her, blocking the heat of the sun, as she waited for more. 'Did you consider that? Even once?'

He wasn't going to beg her to believe him. He'd make her believe him.

CHAPTER SIX

ATHENA WAS EXCRUCIATINGLY aware of the curious gazes of passers-by and wondered where the car was. She'd called the driver the second she'd burst out of the hospital. Her initial plan to return to her villa alone and have some space to think, thwarted as Kostas had marched out to join her.

'Are you claiming Alexio lied?' she asked, unable to stop this conversation even though she knew having it so publicly would almost certainly make the well-known Petrakis family fill the gossip columns for all the wrong reasons. She needed to hear Kostas's side of the events. Now.

Kostas looked at her, the sun in his face, making it almost impossible to read his expression. He used his hand to shield his eyes, but she knew he was glaring at her, that his eyes were full of glittering anger. She could feel it radiating from him, rushing over her like a high tide.

'I'm saying you should have given me – us – a chance.'

Those first doubts clouded back in, forcing her to consider the possibility. Had she wrongly taken Alexio's word over her husband's? She had. Her fear and his sudden need to start a family had both pushed her to that point. She'd used all Alexio had told her, too afraid to admit she wasn't the wife Kostas deserved.

There was one thing she was sure of now, and it was that she hadn't truly known him. Just as he had never discovered the real Athena hiding beneath the surface of a professional and successful woman, she'd never found the real Kostas. But how could she when he'd kept her emotionally at arm's length? Just as her father had done.

Was that where it had all gone wrong for them? That each of them was hiding things – from each other and even themselves?

The car pulled up and Athena breathed a sigh of relief. 'I'm not discussing this here.' She walked to the car, giving Kostas little option but to follow her. Still unable to voice her fears, admit she'd destroyed their marriage all by herself.

The car door shut, and the heat of the afternoon was blocked out. Athena used the cool air conditioning to calm her rattled nerves. This was something they needed to sort out, once and for all. But in the privacy of her villa.

The other door opened, and Kostas sat beside her, the slam of his door loud with a ring finality to it. He was annoyed with her. But her annoyance matched his. She wished he'd defended himself all those months ago. Pain seared through her. Why hadn't he come after her, fought for their marriage – for her?

'It looks very much like you are running away again.'

His voice was hard, his dark eyes boring into hers, demandingly challenging her to do just that.

Well this time he'd be disappointed. This time she had to stay. For her father's sake, they needed to put whatever it was behind them and at least become friends.

Or lovers...

That traitorous thought slipped like a whisper of velvet into her mind.

'I am not running away.' She refuted his accusation with a defiant lift of her chin as she hastily let that thought go. 'I prefer to discuss the intimate details of my marriage in private.'

Kostas laughed softly, sending a tremor of awareness skittering down her spine as the car moved into the traffic. She glanced at the driver. He would be discreet, but still she didn't want to have this conversation until she and Kostas were safely in her villa. Alone.

Kostas glanced at the driver, a smile lingering at the edges of his lips. Already he was teasing her. Using the undeniable attraction still humming between them to his full advantage.

She looked out of the window at the Acropolis high on the hill above Athens. Anywhere other than at Kostas, but her skin tingled and she knew he was watching her, that his eyes were taking in every detail of her body, just as he had done when she'd emerged from his villa guest suite this morning.

'Then that is what we shall do,' Kostas said, and despite herself she turned to look at him, stunned into silence when he reached for her hand, wrapping his own around it.

Warmth skittered through her, filling her with the

same sizzling awareness she'd had the moment she'd seen him swimming in his pool. That was an image she was unable to banish from her mind – her memory.

'We will lock ourselves away until everything is settled between us,' Kostas added, as if to make it clear exactly what he intended.

Her eyes widened in surprise. Everything? Even the explosive passion she knew was building. That wicked lick of desire swirled around inside her, uncurling at the thought of being locked away with him. Why did she want him so much? How could he still fire desire in her veins as if nothing had gone wrong between them?

'And we will stay there until we have agreed how we can give my father what he needs.' She shouldn't have said that. Not when she couldn't keep her part of their deal. It was the attraction. Derailing her and dragging her far from kicking and screaming towards him.

He watched her closely, his eyes focusing on her lips as if he wanted to kiss them. Heat grew deep inside her and she held firm against the urge to slick her tongue over them. Heady sexual tension invaded every corner of the car and she couldn't take her eyes from his face as her heart thudded loudly, desire unravelling itself deep inside her.

Should she just kiss him? Give in to the undeniable need for one another? His eyes darkened and his fingers tightened on her hand. He felt it too. Lust – standing in the way of them sorting things out.

She dragged in a shuddering breath, hating herself for wanting the man she believed had betrayed her so soon after vowing to love her for the rest of his life.

Moments ago, she wanted nothing more than to be in

the sanctuary of her home. To be alone with Kostas to vent her anger, to force the truth from him. Now she didn't trust herself not to fall into his arms and beg him to take her to bed. Because if he looked at her like that any longer, that was exactly what she'd do.

'We will?' he asked seductively and she pressed her lips together in a bid to prevent herself from saying anything.

The car pulled up outside her villa and Athena's relief was so intense she breathed a sigh as Kostas got out of the car. She watched him, tall and lean and incredibly sexy as he walked around the front of the car, taking the time to compose herself. Then he opened her door and reached in to take her hand and help her out.

She ignored it. She couldn't risk the touch of his hand on hers again. It would tip her over the edge. Instead, in a display of what she hoped he would take to be indifference, she got out unaided and walked past him into the villa.

Kostas followed Athena, curious about the villa she now lived in. Unmistakably her design, it reflected her perfectly. His thoughts wandered down that path as he followed her through the villa that wasn't distraction enough from the powerful attraction now surrounding them. That moment in the car had intensified it, leaving his body aching with need for his wife. The urge to move across the car and kiss her – and so much more – had been so intense, but he'd fought it. Hard.

He wasn't about to allow lust to distract him, pass up the opportunity she'd given him to clear his name, at least in her eyes. Athena had to know how her brother had manipulated her, destroying their marriage because of his intense jealousy for Kostas.

Athena stood by the window, looking out to the far distance, as if the sea on the horizon would calm the fire that he knew was on the verge of erupting inside her.

She didn't turn to him as he moved closer. Her arms were folded, and he knew her lips would be pressed together in a firm line of annoyance. Maybe it was just as well he couldn't see her because he'd be far too tempted to kiss that annoyance away. To give in to the desire that at this very moment was dangerously entwined with anger.

'Why would he do that to me?' Athena's voice was brittle as if she was biting back the anger. Or was it the passion?

Kostas swallowed hard, trying to dislodge the sickening sensation of betraying Alexio in his throat. Hell, that man didn't deserve such considerations.

'To compromise me.' He saw Athena's shoulders stiffen as he spoke, and curled his fingers into tight fists to stop himself from reaching for her. Pride wouldn't allow him to beg.

Finally, she was beginning to see for herself that he'd never betrayed her, that it was her brother who was guilty of that charge. A man who was no longer here to speak for himself – or anyone else. Pride and the love he'd once had for Athena also prevented Kostas from tarnishing the memory of her brother. If she accepted what her brother was really like, it would be because she'd come to that conclusion all by herself.

Athena turned to face him. 'But ...' She paused,

blinking as she looked at him, as if she knew the answer to the question she hadn't yet asked. 'Alexio lied?'

The lie that had been the catalyst to end his marriage. But it was his wife's lack of faith in him, lack of trust, that had destroyed it, he reminded himself, seeing the vulnerability on Athena's face as she waited for his answer.

He said nothing. Waiting. Hoping she would see the truth for herself.

'Alexio. My own brother.' Her voice was barely more than a whisper as she said her brother's name, and relief swept through him that he didn't have to openly accuse her brother. A man she'd clearly adored and sadly, due to his wild ways, now mourned by her and Sebastianos. But the old man had always had the measure of his son. Always known he hadn't wanted to settle to adult life and the responsibilities of the family business.

Sebastianos had known how jealous Alexio was of Kostas.

'I'm sorry.' His apology slipped out, inadvertently confirming her suspicions.

'No, he wouldn't.'

'I know he was your brother and that you've lost him far too early, but he wasn't a saint, Athena.'

Athena let out a sob as she flopped down onto the chair, her elbows on her lap, her head hanging down, dark hair cascading around her face. She looked broken.

Kostas gritted his teeth together against the urge to go to her and offer comfort. It surged over him like a herd of wild animals and he didn't dare touch her. If he did, there could be no knowing what would happen next.

She dragged in a shuddering breath. 'So am I.' She

looked up at him, her eyes moist with tears. 'Why didn't you say something? Defend yourself? Was our marriage so unimportant to you that you couldn't fight for it?'

Even though he knew it was a mistake, he lowered himself down in front of her and took her hands between his, feeling the band of gold on her right hand. He looked into her eyes, to the soft brown swimming with unshed tears, and his heart wrenched open, threatening to set free all he'd locked away when she'd walked out on him.

'You are the one who walked away, Athena. It is you who gave up on our marriage.' Her eyes searched his and he hated himself for inflicting this pain, for making this fake reconciliation harder for her, but pride was a hard obstacle to overcome. 'You destroyed everything we had.'

'If you feel that, why did you even come back to Athens with me?' Those sensuously soft eyes implored him to open up to her, to let her in.

He sighed and, despite everything, felt the door to his past creaking slowly open. 'Because I owe your father.'

'I know all that,' she said softly, confusion furrowing her brows. 'He helped you start your business, gave you the chance nobody else ever had.'

Kostas shook his head slowly. 'It's more than that. He believed in me and became the father figure I had never known.'

Realisation slowly slipped over Athena's face, wiping away the confusion. 'Alexio wasn't just jealous of your success, was he?'

Again he shook his head, relieved he wasn't having to spell any of this out to her, but annoyed she'd taken so long to realise it. So long that it was now too late for their marriage – for them. He'd locked his love away, reverted to being the man he'd been before they'd dated. A man who felt totally unworthy of a woman like Athena.

He had to accept they needed to go their separate ways. That the marriage had been based purely on passion, which alone wasn't enough to hold it together. But he couldn't yet. He wouldn't ever marry again. Of that he was certain. He'd never have the opportunity to have a legitimate heir, be better than his father.

For that reason alone, the deal he and Athena had made beside his pool yesterday morning had to stand, even though he hated the callousness of his demand and despised the man she'd made him become.

'He hated that Father looked on you as a son, even before we married.' Again, Athena prevented him from damning her brother.

'He did, yes.' Kostas watched Athena, seeing realisation sinking in.

She drew in another ragged breath, close to tears. 'And he couldn't stand it that I loved you.'

'That's true.' Kostas finally found his voice.

Her eyes searched his and her lips parted. 'And I ...' Her words faltered, and she looked down at their hands entwined. She pulled hers free of his, looking back up at him, her hand moving to his face, her palm resting against his cheek.

He didn't move. Painfully aware of the thud of his heart as she touched him so affectionately, the way she'd always done before she kissed him. If she kissed him now...

'I let you down,' she whispered, her hand pressing against his face.

She moved towards him and he held his breath. He

wanted her lips on his, wanted her kiss. Damn it he wanted to kiss her back. Set free the passion and desire that had never gone away. His whole body was full of it now. But she'd called it lust. Denied it was anything else.

As if in slow motion she moved towards him and brushed her lips lightly over his, her eyes fluttering closed. He remained firm and rigid against the onslaught in his body and the powerful urge to respond, because he couldn't do that. They didn't belong to one another and he most certainly didn't deserve her.

He was nothing. A nobody who'd come from nothing. Her kiss of sympathy unleashed the hurt and angry boy he'd once been. The boy who'd been forced to steal food just to stave off hunger. That boy mixed with the fiercely proud man he'd become.

He didn't want her sympathy. He wanted what they'd had before she'd doubted him. A place they could never go back to.

Athena pulled back, pale with shock. He sensed her unease, her doubt.

Kostas stood up and moved away from her, from the temptation that feather-light kiss had provoked. Was he right to make such outrageous demands of her? How could that ever lead them back to what they'd had? 'We have much to settle before we embark on keeping your side of the deal.'

Anger obliterated the passion, cooling the desire and even though he knew his words were harsh, he couldn't keep them in. It was his defence, his way of keeping all he'd once felt for her safely locked away.

. . .

'Is that all you can think about?' Sickness rushed over Athena, filling her tummy, killing the butterflies as if snow had fallen and frozen them stiff.

'Our deal,' he said with a self-assured flick of his brow, 'Is the reason I am here. The reason you came to me in Crete.'

The truth of his words cut deep. For a moment back there she'd almost given into the urge to taste the desire which sparked so uncontrollably between them. To satisfy it – and her body – so that they could concentrate on portraying the image of a couple reunited.

Now stark reality was back in focus. So clear it sparkled like a crystal. Kostas didn't love her anymore. His warning that she should have believed the man who had loved her had been past tense. And just now, he hadn't wanted to indulge in that chemistry he'd once found so irresistible. Was he trying to prove he could hold out against such powerful sexual tension? That no matter what, he wouldn't indulge in even a kiss?

She watched Kostas stride across the room. He sat down on the sofa, his arm outstretched along the back of it, as if he were open and relaxed. He was anything but.

'It is,' she agreed, trying to deal with the hurt of his rejection. Never before had he denied her a kiss, rejected her so coldly. 'And I came because my father believes you have a duty to him. A debt.' She stood up and crossed the room, away from the sunlight and towards the sofa where Kostas sat, looking as if they were merely talking about the weather. 'And I think it's about time you told me just what that is.'

'Isn't that what I have just done?' His dark eyes fixed on her, but she remained tall and in control. She would not allow him to see how his rejection stung. How it made her feel like shutting herself away and crying for the love she'd destroyed by using Alexio's jealousy as a shield for her fear.

She pushed aside her brother's treachery and focused on her husband. He was the key to giving her father back his spark, his fight, and no matter what, she had to keep him here, keep him onside.

But what of his terms? No, she couldn't allow herself to worry about that. The only thing that was important now was clearing the air between them so that they could portray the image of lovers at Phoebe's name day party in just five days' time. A show of reunited love for all the family to see.

'No. As ever, you have kept who you really are in the shadows.' Hurt made her words ring with it.

Kostas sat forwards on the sofa and looked up at her. 'I grew up like a stray dog,' he said harshly and the image that flew into her mind made her heart ache for the young boy he must have been. He'd already proved he no longer wanted her sympathy, her affection, but she couldn't keep it at bay.

'Every day was a fight for survival. My mother spent most of her time drunk or hungover and as for my father...'

He looked at her and swallowed hard. She stood waiting, not daring to say anything that would break the honest flow from his past.

'He didn't bother to stick around to see me grow up. He didn't even have the guts to marry my mother when she became pregnant, and that destroyed her. If I ever set eyes on him again, it will be too soon.' The hatred and venom in those words was so agonizing she gasped in shock.

He looked at her, but he wasn't seeing her anymore. He was lost in the pain of an experience no child should endure. Her heart hammered and the need to go to him, to touch him, bring him back from that terrible memory she'd unwittingly unlocked was so fierce, she had to press her fingernails into her palms. The pain didn't come anywhere close to matching his. But it helped her stay silent – and still.

'As I grew up, I scavenged almost every bit of food I ate.' His lips curled into a snarl, as if he'd become the stray dog he'd likened himself to. 'But still my mother drank. Ultimately it killed her.'

Athena remained silent; the rays of afternoon sun had moved across the room and now shone on Kostas, making this painful moment of truth more surreal.

'I was seventeen when she died and glad of it. I was free.'

Athena bit her lower lip, trying to stifle a gasp and the pain filling her for the man she'd fallen in love with. Why had he never trusted her enough to confide in her? Because he hadn't loved her enough?

He looked at her, his eyes focused on her, as if he were returning from the hell that had been his childhood. 'I despise myself for that.'

'Kostas,' she said, wishing he'd accept her support.

'I met Elias when I was young. His childhood hadn't been much better.' He clenched his fingers together as he sat just like she had. She wanted to kneel in front of him, hold his hands as he'd done to her, but unlike him, she didn't want to do it out of duty.

Something else drove her. Something she wasn't ready to admit to. Especially after he'd just rejected her so coldly.

'And my father was the only man who'd given you a chance.' She said the part of his story she already knew, wondering just how much of what he'd told her, her father knew. Was that why he welcomed him into the family, treated him like a son? Because Kostas's father had turned his back on him?

'Do you know where your father is?'

Kostas looked up at her, his expression making it clear he realised where her mind had taken her. 'I don't. And I never want to speak of him again, let alone find the selfish bastard.'

Athena could hardly contain her relief that they were finally opening up to one another, revealing who they really were. Or at least he was. Kostas's lips twitched in a smile, making him look more like the man she'd confronted yesterday beside his pool.

He shook his head. 'You believed all Alexio told you, which makes your opinion of me so low, you think I would marry you for material gain.'

Hostilities were back. The good allowing him to talk had achieved had been undone.

'No. That's not what went wrong.' Hotly she defended herself, their marriage. 'But it feels like you married me because of my father.'

'Because he treated me like a son?'

'Yes.' The word settled between them.

'You jumped to conclusions.' Kostas looked at her, annoyance taking away any trace of the man he'd always been at pains to hide from. 'Conclusions fuelled by lies.'

'I'm sorry. I've apologised.' She looked at him, annoyed at how unmoved he now was, how shut off. 'And just now, I tried to... wanted to...'

'Kiss me.' He cut her words off brutally.

Shame burned her cheeks. Why had she even thought that giving in to the desire she'd felt between them would be helpful? Such an action could never make their situation any less complicated. She couldn't defend herself.

'That was just lust.' He flung her words back at her and she inhaled deeply, desperate not to react to the indignation.

'Where does that leave us now?' She had to sort this out. For her father's sake. In less than a week, they would be on parade as a loving couple and her father would be waiting to hear from other family members that this was the case.

'Back where we started.' Kostas stood up and pulled off his tie, winding it around his hand.

For a moment she was transfixed by the action. Something she'd seen him do many times when they were first married, but suddenly now seemed so sexy. So intimate.

'We still have a deal?' she asked carefully. There was much at stake here. She needed Kostas for her father's sake, even though ultimately she could lose everything.

'We do, but right now, I need a shower.'

Athena's pulse leapt at the thought of Kostas in the shower, at the memories of the times they'd taken a shower together. Of water sluicing over their bodies as they'd made love. Heady desire that had swept her away...

She slammed those thoughts away. 'Then I will leave you in peace to do just that.'

'You are not joining me?'

Athena blinked as Kostas smiled at her. A smile that didn't reach his eyes, didn't give any hint of passion. Only provocation.

'In the interests of ensuring our fake reconciliation looks real?' she asked light-heartedly, acutely aware of the thudding of her heart and the swell of need low down in her pelvis.

Damn him.

'Or maybe out of sympathy.' His words dropped like ice cubes into a glass, hurtling downward fast before rising back up. 'Or is it just kisses you offer as sympathy?'

Retaliation was on the tip of her tongue, but she fought the urge. 'I have far more important things to attend to in my office. Shower alone and for as long as you wish. I will see you for dinner this evening.'

Without waiting for his reply, Athena turned and left him, heading for her office. She wanted to be on her own, to lick the wounds inflicted on her by her husband's rejection and reflect on the shocking truth of his childhood and her brother's betrayal. A betrayal that had cost her marriage.

CHAPTER SEVEN

KOSTAS HAD STOOD under the cold jets of the shower until he'd shivered, but still the slug of desire persisted. The memory of his childhood hadn't been washed away either, it lingered over him like an impending storm, reminding him all through dinner with Athena that he didn't deserve her or her father's respect.

'Did you finish your work?' Kostas asked as they entered the more intimate living room which adjoined her bedroom and the guest room he'd been allocated, glad he could stop the pretence of mindless conversation they'd conducted throughout their meal. He'd barely tasted the souvlaki and as for the fine wine, it had done nothing to dull the way just looking at Athena aroused his body.

And why shouldn't he? She was his wife. His vibrant sexy wife.

It's just lust.

Again, her declaration of what was between them when she'd stood beside his pool overrode everything.

'Yes, I did,' she said softly as she walked into the dimly lit room, the soft cream silk of her dress accentuating every curve. She stood and faced him, the backdrop of Athens in the distance beyond the floor-to-ceiling windows, giving her a goddess-like appearance.

'I think we should visit your father tomorrow, then go out. We need to be seen in public to build up the story of our reunion before the party,' he said into the silence which was rapidly filling with that explosive sexual chemistry again.

'I have too much work to go out and build up the façade of reunion.' Athena looked at him, the fast rise and fall of her breasts making it more than obvious she too felt the sexual tension – or lust as she preferred to call it. 'It's better if we just visit Father.'

Each breath she took increased the need in his body, and he couldn't help but look at her breasts, delicately outlined beneath the silk. Inwardly he groaned as his body responded.

'You can't hide behind work forever, Athena,' Kostas said firmly. Wasn't that exactly what he'd done as their marriage had started to show its weaknesses? Remaining later and later at the office, avoiding her and his emotions?

'I'm not the only one who hides behind work.' The tart reply confirmed his question so succinctly. 'We are both guilty of that.'

Kostas watched her as she walked to the floor-to-ceiling windows, looking out into the darkness. 'What is it you are hiding from now?'

She turned to face him, folding her arms in front of her. 'The truth.' She took a deep breath and walked back into the room. Her gaze met his and for the first time ever, he felt as if he was looking right into her heart. He held his breath, sensing there was more, that silence and patience were all she needed to unlock the door she'd slammed in his face.

'What is that truth?' he asked gently.

'That I am nothing in my father's eyes.'

Kostas bit down hard at the pain in her voice. Was that why she'd achieved so much? First-class honours in her degree, lucrative contract after contract when she'd joined Petrakis Enterprises and the award for her architectural designs since she'd left him? To prove herself to her father?

How could she think that?

'Your father adores you.'

Athena looked at him, disappointment filling her beautiful face. 'As a daughter maybe, but as someone to work alongside him, to take his business into the future...' Her words trailed off and she shook her head, looking down at the floor. When she looked back up, she was biting her lip.

'Then you must show him,' Kostas said, unsure how to deal with this sudden revelation. It wasn't what he'd expected at all. Behind her façade of being career driven she'd been hiding not just from all that was wrong in their relationship, but from the one with her father.

'I don't know how to,' she said, a hint of resignation in her voice which cut deep into him. Deeper than he'd ever thought possible. Where was her strength? Her determination?

'I will do everything I can to ensure your father believes in our reconciliation, but you must show him who you really are.' The look in Kostas's eyes definitely unnerved Athena. He was asking her to come out from behind her barriers.

If she did, would she reveal her true self to him in the process? And in turn, would he have to show who he really was? Athena blinked in confusion and that wrench in his heart happened again. Lust, he reminded himself. Nothing but lust.

'Do you think that will be sufficient?' She kicked off first one heeled shoe, and then the other, taking him back to the days of their marriage. Then she'd always looked at him with sultry passion in her eyes, asking him without words to take her to bed and make love to her. Now it was as if she wanted to go back to that, as if she'd forgotten the barrier between them.

He drew in a sharp breath and let it out, causing Athena to look abruptly at him. 'It will. The sooner your father believes we are together, the sooner he can fight his way back to health. Then you can show him what you can bring to Petrakis Enterprises and more.'

Sadness flickered over her face, vulnerability showing in her eyes. She looked down at her discarded shoes. Again, echoes of their marriage filled his mind and he fought the urge to go to her, to turn her and slide the zip of her dress down as he'd done many times in their short marriage.

'Yes, it will,' Kostas said as she turned from him again and stood looking at the view. He remained where he was, looking at a different view. He wasn't the slightest bit interested in Athens, lit up in the distance. Or the fact that the modern villa had unrivalled views from its vantage point on the hillside.

All he had eyes for was Athena.

His body was on full alert and he hadn't so much as touched her. Was this what abstinence did, or was this what his wife did to him?

She looked at the clock on the wall. 'It's getting late.'

'Then I should say goodnight.' It was the last thing he wanted.

She turned to look at him, biting her lower lip. 'Stay a little longer,' she whispered.

He moved closer to her, keeping his hands firmly at his sides. 'Do you want me to stay?'

She nodded. 'This feels like those nights after we married.' She stopped, as if aware she was giving herself away.

'When I would unfasten your dress?' Hell, but he wanted to do that. The air around them sizzled with tension as she looked at him without saying anything. The darkness of her eyes confirming she wanted that as much as he did. But if anything happened, it had to be her choice, not because he'd instigated anything.

'I could forget anything then,' she whispered, looking at him from lowered lashes, the invitation of doing that right now lingering in the air.

'Anything.' His hoarse agreement only added to the building tension.

Athena reached behind her and began to fumble with the zip of her dress, her breathing deep, and her eyes even darker as she watched him. She'd always turned her back to him, lifted her hair from her neck and waited for him to pull down the zip on her dress. She blinked, dragging in a ragged breath, her invitation clear. Did she have any idea what she was doing to him?

Slowly she turned and he closed his eyes against the powerful jolt of desire rushing through him. Without realising he'd moved, he was behind her, putting his fingers over hers. Instantly she stilled and he waited, his heart thudding, blood pounding through every part of his body.

'Kostas,' she whispered, her hands covered by his.

'I want you to forget everything. Just as you used to.' His voice was deep and hoarse, the power of the moment getting the better of him, making his heart thud wildly with anticipation.

'I want to, but ...' Her whispered words died out and he waited, every nerve in his body tuned into her.

'But what, Athena?'

'We should be talking, not giving in to this need.'

'We don't have to talk right now,' he whispered, willing her to move her hands, give him consent to help her unzip her dress as he'd done so many times before. 'Actions can be louder. They can speak volumes.'

He swallowed down the sigh of relief as she slowly moved her hands from beneath his and lifted her hair up. Her slender neck as sexy as he'd remembered, making him harder than he'd ever been.

Slowly, gently, he eased the zip of her dress down, exposing her back, the cream lace of her bra adding to the thrill of finally touching her like he'd done before...

No, he wouldn't go there now. He wanted to savour this moment. Make it as special, as arousing as possible for Athena. Show her they could be good together. That they could forget anything. Even if it was only for a moment out of time and driven by lust.

He took the zip all the way down to her waist and she

remained still. Was this an invitation to take it further?

Tentatively he reached to the top of her back, then trailed the tip of his finger down her spine. She softly sighed, her back arching slightly away from his touch as he moved back to her waist.

'I've always loved kissing the back of your neck. Can I?' His hoarse whisper sought her consent to continue with the torture he was inflicting on himself. If she wanted him to stop, he would. It would kill him, but he would.

'Yes.' Her husky agreement pushed him almost to the edge of his endurance. His body ached for her. Ached for the pleasure and satisfaction of being inside her. Deep inside her.

He wanted – no, needed to reclaim his wife.

He moved his face closer to her neck, inhaling the scent of her light floral perfume mingling with the fresh smell of apple shampoo in her hair. He wanted to devour her, but he wasn't going to rush this moment. He wanted to savour every second of it.

He blew very softly at the nape of her neck, the soft sigh which slipped from her only adding to the intensity of his need. Her breathing deepened and he wasn't even touching her – yet. The anticipation was as wild for her as it was for him.

He resisted the urge to slide her dress from her shoulders as he'd done so often, instead he pressed his lips teasingly to where he'd just breathed on her skin. Then he tasted her, and memories collided with the heady need of right now.

'You taste delicious,' he whispered so close to her skin that it was like a kiss.

Athena moaned softly with pleasure and although he didn't think it was possible, he grew harder still, his trousers straining against him.

Wanting to continue the torture, he lowered himself, sliding his tongue down the same trail his finger had just taken, all the way to her waist. The effort of not taking her hips in his hands as he went as low as he could go, almost too much, and he groaned.

'Oh,' she gasped in a whisper as her body began to writhe slowly against the onslaught of pleasure. 'Kostas.'

His name on her lips made him smile and he kissed her lower back, then trailed his lips up to the nape of her neck again.

She turned to face him, her eyes wide and filled with desire, her lips parted, inviting his kiss. He reached out to touch her throat, watching her delicately swallow as his fingers hovered over her skin.

'I want to touch you,' he whispered huskily. 'Fill your sexy body with desire.'

She blinked, as if in a foggy haze of desire. 'Touch me,' she whispered, watching him with eyes so large, so dark, it gave her an alluring innocence.

He placed his fingertip at the cusp of her throat, keeping his focus on where he was touching her, aware of her watching him. Slowly he trailed his finger towards her collarbone and onto the cream silk of her dress, so fine it offered little barrier against his touch.

As his finger trailed lower, towards the softness of her breast, her nipples peaked against the silk. He continued his torment – of himself as well as her – trailing his finger lower, pausing on the hardness of her nipple, circling it.

She drew in a breath, held it as his finger moved

around the hardened peak once more, before moving lower, pressing softly underneath the fullness of her breast. Then lower, down her flat tummy and still lower until his finger met the subtle line of her panties beneath her dress.

He looked up at her, his desire so intense he couldn't smile, such was the control he was inflicting on himself. Still maintaining the contact with the pad of his finger, he lowered to his knees before her and began trailing his finger down to the top of her thigh. So close to the most intimate part of her.

Not yet, he reprimanded himself as his finger paused, the temptation of moving towards that part of her so great he clenched his jaw hard. He looked up as Athena bent her head forward, her hair sliding bit by bit from her shoulders to form a sexy curtain of silk.

For a moment he thought she was going to reach out and push her fingers into his hair. Her fingers flexed and a smile twitched on his lips. She was fighting it as hard as he was.

He resumed his trail, moving his finger down her thigh, towards the hem of her dress and onto her knee. The softness of her bare leg so different to the silk of her dress. Still he trailed his finger lower, down the front of her leg, onto her foot and then to her painted toenails.

He sat back, agonisingly hard as he looked up at her. She was trembling, her lips parted and her eyes intensely dark with desire.

'That,' she whispered as her eyes met his. 'That was...' Again, she paused, as if she couldn't form the words, as if desire had robbed her of the ability to say anything. 'So nice I forgot everything.'

Kostas slowly got to his feet, standing close to her, so close that he could easily cover her lips with his, easily take this gentle teasing moment to another level. One where restraint and control would be unleashed and he could thrust into her, deep into her, as she writhed naked beneath him, calling out his name.

That was his usual style. What he'd just done to Athena, he'd never done to any woman before and it was nice, as she'd called it. It was also incredibly erotic and tantalising doing that to her. Teasing her – and himself.

Making them both wait.

'More?' he asked softly, looking into the depths of her eyes as she looked up at him. In the almost blackness they now were in, he saw innocence, vulnerability, and something else. Then her long lashes fluttered down, and she closed her eyes.

'More,' she whispered her agreement, eyes remaining closed. He reached out his other hand, wanting to trace that erotic trail on the other side of her body with his other finger.

Athena held her breath. Wanting everything to remain forgotten. Waiting for his touch. When it came it was far more intense than moments before and she kept her eyes closed, using her other senses. Hearing him breathing, deep and hard. Smelling his cologne, spicy and fresh. Anticipating the taste of his lips on hers. Feeling his finger as he moved it slowly in a circle at the base of her throat.

How could that be so wildly exciting?

She swallowed hard, then drew in a ragged breath,

keeping her eyes closed as she lifted her chin as if looking up at him, a smile of pure contentment on her lips.

'Keep your eyes closed.' Kostas whispered his command hoarsely, heavy with desire.

She smiled as a tremor of pleasure skittered down her spine. 'I intend to.'

This time, instead of trailing to her right collarbone, his finger trailed over the skin in the other direction. A soft sigh escaped her parted lips as she realised he was going to do the same again on the other side of her body.

The suspense was almost too much. Their love-making had always been intense, with a reckless abandon and impatience. But this was wildly erotic. A pulse of desire throbbed between her legs and her body ached for more than just the trailing touch of his fingertip.

He was the one touching her, yet she felt the one in control and command of the moment. The one who could stop it – if she wanted to. But she didn't want this moment to end.

Her breasts ached for his touch as his fingertip moved onto the silk of her dress at her shoulder. The silence of the room was full of tension and anticipation. She kept her eyes closed while he trailed lower towards her other breast. She drew in another ragged breath as he moved onto her other breast and towards her nipple which she knew would be so hard it would be peaking against her bra and the fine cream silk of her dress. Would he notice how very aroused she was?

She bit her lower lip. She hoped so.

The trail moved to the firmness of her breast and she held her breath as his finger trailed over her breast. She let out a shaky exhale, then groaned as he circled her nipple. The need to open her eyes, to look at the inky blackness of his, so full of desire, was almost too much.

Her breathing became shallow pants as he continued the torture, slowly, and so deliciously. She bit her lower lip as his fingertip slid lower then moved away.

She was trembling. Her whole body aroused to his touch. Waiting for more. Wanting more.

The trail moved lower, down over her tummy. She clenched herself as the insatiable desire to feel him touch her intimately burned at the very core of her. She heard his soft, low laugh. A sound so sexy, so wild and erotic she almost opened her eyes.

'Eyes closed,' he whispered, and she knew he was watching her face, seeing her every reaction to his touch as his finger trailed lower in its torturous trail. He was revelling in his power over her. And she relished it as if she'd just been rescued from the heart of a desert and he was water.

She heard him lower himself to his knees, just as he'd done last time. Then, she'd looked down at him, holding out against the urge to plunge her fingers into the thickness of his hair. Instead she'd looked down at the man, if truth be told – accepting, she was still very much in love with. The evidence of how much he wanted her, the hardness of his erection, she'd have been blind not to notice.

Instinctively, she knew his need of her was the same now and she pressed her palms against her hips, desperate to stop herself reaching for him, tousling her fingers into his hair as she'd always done when he took her to that wonderfully passionate place.

Except they'd never been here before...

She gasped as his fingertip moved away from the expected trail, heading for the boiling point of her desire. His touch moved slowly over her tummy, along the top of line of her panties, then paused in the middle. Her hips moved towards him with an eagerness that shocked and excited her as his fingertip felt like a feather moving lower and lower.

She let out a breath she hadn't realised she'd been holding as he moved away, back to mirror the actions he'd followed last time and then slowly down her thigh. She was trembling so much now, she thought she might collapse beneath the weight of the desire which was almost at exploding point inside her.

His finger continued the torture, moving slowly lower and when he touched the bare skin of her knee, she couldn't keep the moan of pleasure in. Her head tipped back, her eyes closed, as he trailed down the front of her leg and to her foot, reaching her toes.

How could that be so exciting, so...

The torture, the exquisite pleasure ended, and she heard him move. Was he sitting back, looking up at her as he'd done last time? Did she dare look down at him?

'Is that lust?' The whispered question took her by surprise and she opened her eyes and she looked down at him. He was sitting just as before, looking up at her and hugely aroused.

Lust? Was it lust when he'd just scorched into her body, bringing her to the realisation that her lust could be love? That if she were brave enough, she'd admit she still loved him. That she always had done and that she'd run – left him, because she loved him so much. Not because she'd believed he'd betrayed her by seeing another woman. Because she knew she couldn't ever give him what she'd discovered he wanted.

But she wasn't brave enough to do it. Not when he'd made it clear he didn't love her. And when she called the attraction, the desire which had surged through them within seconds of her arriving at his villa in Crete, lust, hadn't he agreed? Or at least he hadn't denied it.

She nodded her head slowly. 'Yes,' she breathed. 'Lust.'

He nodded too. 'Then lust will make it so very pleasurable to create our baby.'

Athena drew in a sharp breath, as if someone had thrown an ice-cold bucket of water over her. No, not a bucket. A whole lake. She struggled for breath, blinking against the shock.

Create our baby.

Panic surged through her, obliterating every last drop of the pleasure and desire he'd inflicted on her. Crashing her down from the heights he'd taken her to – with just the touch of his fingertip.

She stepped back from him, shaking her head in denial, unable to speak, aware he was now on his feet, moving towards her. She continued to shake her head, faster, and put out her hands, her palms making contact with his chest.

'No. No, I can't.' She found her voice, but it was more like a strangled cry. She trembled, no longer with desire, but with fear. Icy cold fear. It was more than her fear of being a mother, it was a fear that had become so much more as she'd grown up.

'Athena?' She heard the question in her name, the confusion. Felt him press against her palms, his arms go around her, trying to hold her. She pushed against him. Hard.

'I can't.' She shook her head, painfully aware she must look petrified. She was petrified. She couldn't put into words how she felt, even to herself. So how could she ever being to explain it to Kostas?

'Can't what?' he demanded. She had to stop this. Should never have allowed that moment of intimacy to happen. Not when she knew she'd never be able to meet his terms, that just doing so would be to condemn herself to more torture, more heartache.

'Can't what, Athena?' Kostas demanded, the softness of moments ago obliterated.

'Have a baby,' she almost cried out the words at him.

Kostas was stunned into inaction and silence. What the hell had just happened? How had Athena gone from a purring kitten to a cornered wildcat within seconds – after what they'd just shared? The intimacy hadn't made them forget this time. It had brought something dark to the surface.

'Why not?' he asked, unsure where this had come from.

She was shaking. Not trembling with desire as she had been moments ago but shaking – with fear. He searched her face for answers, finding none. What had he done? What had changed her so dramatically? He wasn't demanding collection of his terms now. All he'd wanted was to give her pleasure. Find their way back to where they'd been before she'd walked out. Pave a new path back to passion. But they'd taken a wrong turn somewhere.

'Because I'm scared to.' Her eyes were wide with fear, panic resounding in her words. He stepped back, giving her space.

'Scared of what?' He raked his hand through his hair, unable to follow the bizarre twist to the evening. 'Me?'

She shook her head firmly, her hair flinging out with the movement.

'Then what?' Frustration made the words hard, his voice demanding. He didn't know what the hell was going on.

'What you want.' She gulped down hard and through the angry frustration something else flickered to life deep inside him, tugging at his heart, threatening to open the door to the love he'd once had for Athena.

'What I want is to give my wife pleasure and when the time is right, I want to have sex with her.' It was impossible to keep the annoyance, the frustration, from his voice. 'Why does that scare you?'

'Not that,' she almost wailed, the sound so primal, so distressing he felt his eyes widen in surprise.

'Then what?' he demanded, confusion making the words hard.

'A baby.'

'A baby?' Kostas was totally confused – totally out of his depth.

He watched as all the fight drained from Athena and her eyes brimmed with tears. Fear spiked at him.

'I'm scared – petrified – of the thought of carrying and giving birth to a baby.'

CHAPTER EIGHT

FOR THE FIRST time in her life, Athena had told someone her darkest, most severe fear and not just the worry which neatly wrapped her inner turmoil. The whole thing. Now she felt exposed. Vulnerable.

She searched Kostas's face, desperate to see his reaction but dreading it at the same time. She couldn't give him what he wanted. Couldn't keep her side of their deal, but her mind was dragged so far back into the past she couldn't even worry about the implications of what she was telling him.

Her heart thudded in her chest, but not with the desire he'd brought to life within her just with the simplest of actions. It hammered with absolute and complete panic. She could hear it thumping in her ears, feel the terror racing in her veins. What if he dismissed it as something trivial? Just as she'd been doing to herself for so long.

But it wasn't trivial. Her fear of pregnancy was as real as Kostas was standing before her now. So real and so very frightening that she'd never sought advice, never even searched the internet to see if it was something other women experienced. Doing that would mean facing it and that was the one thing she'd avoided – until the day she'd known her marriage was over. The day Kostas had announced he was ready for fatherhood.

Now, his almost throwaway remark about creating their baby had triggered all that anxiety and more. She swallowed down hard and looked at him, bracing herself for... what she didn't know.

'Why. Athena?' he asked firmly, his brow furrowed in concern and confusion. 'What happened to make you afraid of something so natural?'

Athena's mind spun back and as she stood there looking at Kostas, she could feel herself being drawn away from him, down the dark foreboding passage and back to the night she'd been alone in the house with her mother. The night her mother, with her belly bulging in a way that had frightened Athena, had writhed on her bed in the pain of labour. The night her mother, and her baby sister, had been dying from complications.

She'd been powerless to help, unable to soothe her mother's pain, let alone save her.

'Mother died giving birth when I was a young girl.' She couldn't find a voice for the whole story yet, but it was a relief to finally be able to tell someone. To have opened a door that had hidden the horror of that night behind it for many years. Now those demons were trying to force themselves out and take over. Trying to destroy her dreams.

Destroying her.

After Alexio's death, she was all too aware that only

she could continue the family. But she'd never be able to be more than just a daughter to her father. He had only ever seen his son as the future of his empire and that would never change, even if she achieved the almost impossible and had a son.

And if she didn't, would Kostas take everything she'd worked so hard for? Her father could hand it all over to him without the slightest doubt because he looked upon him as a son. His replacement heir.

Kostas's face was solemn, his lips set in a thin annoyed line. He was angry with her, angry that she was telling him she couldn't keep her part of the deal.

Without a word, he turned from her and walked towards the tray of drinks. Crystal chinked against crystal as he set out two tumblers. She watched in a daze as he picked up the bottle of brandy and poured the dark liquid into each glass. He put the bottle down, picked up the glasses and came back to her.

She hadn't moved. She hadn't been able to. She was locked in a panic that would only go away if she finally told the whole story. And Kostas was the person who needed to hear it. He needed to know she wasn't backing out of their deal lightly, that to be a mother, even though it was her most secret desire, was the one thing she couldn't do.

To be a mother, she needed to have a baby. To be pregnant and give birth. She needed to be strong because her fear of pregnancy had become so much more. What if she had a daughter? Would that little girl be as inconsequential as she was in the eyes of the men who meant the most to her?

She shuddered as icy fingers of dread wrapped around

her, closing her eyes against the pain of the memory, the image forever burned into her mind of her mother, screaming out in pain as what she now knew was another contraction wracked her body.

When she opened her eyes again, Kostas was standing in front of her, a glass of brandy in each hand. Silently he handed her a glass. She was back to the beginning. Back to the moment when the desire he'd filled her with had been obliterated by his casual comment about creating their baby. At the point of facing her fear.

'Drink.' The command in his voice was clear and she welcomed it. She wanted someone to take care of her, to help her through this. Not someone. She wanted Kostas to be there with her because she couldn't shut the door on this memory now. And hadn't he shared his past, his demons? Didn't she owe it to him to tell him the real reason she could never be the mother of his child?

The real reason she'd walked out on him.

She watched as he drank the fiery liquid in one go then sipped hers gingerly. She wasn't a brandy drinker.

'Drink,' he said. 'It will help with the shock.'

'I'm not in shock.'

'You are shaking like a delicate flower in a gale, and I don't care what you say, you are in shock. Drink.'

She put the glass to her lips again and took another sip. Kostas watched her intently and she took another, then another, feeling the heat of the fiery liquid slipping around her body even before she'd finished the last sip.

He took her empty glass from her and turned to place them by the bottle. For a moment, she thought he was going to pour more, but he didn't. He turned and came back to her, took her elbow gently in his hand and drew her towards the sofa.

'Sit down.' There it was again, that total command and right now it was exactly what she needed.

She blinked as he picked up the soft throw and wrapped it around her, before sitting next to her. All she could do was look expectantly at him. She couldn't say anything, couldn't bring that horrifying night out into the present, even though it lingered in the shadows, pressing down on her.

'Your mother died in childbirth when you were but a child yourself. That much I am aware of, but there is more, isn't there, Athena? Much more.'

His words were firm, decisive, and silently she thanked him for being calm, for not arguing with her that she'd made a deal with him, a deal she couldn't keep. It felt like he cared.

'Tell me.' He nudged her mind back to the terror she'd just unleashed. The fear she couldn't pack away again. Not until she'd faced both head on.

She took a deep breath. 'I was ten years old. Mother and I were alone. We lived in a villa miles and miles from Athens, then. Or at least, that was how it had felt that night. I hated the place after that and was so glad when father built his new villa.'

'The villa doesn't matter,' Kostas prompted, bringing her back on course. 'What happened, Athena?'

'We were alone. Father was in Athens and the baby wasn't meant to arrive for another month. She should have been a June baby.' Athena looked at Kostas, an overwhelming sensation of sadness flooding through her, chasing the brandy. 'It was only May. Early May.'

Kostas took her hand as she paused and looked at him. She hoping that was enough, but knew it was far from it.

'Go on,' he urged gently. So gently he almost sounded loving. Like the Kostas he'd been when they'd first known one another and during those first heady weeks of marriage. Before Alexio had destroyed it. Before she'd allowed him to. 'Athena, you need to talk about it.'

She looked at him. 'I can't.'

He squeezed her hand a little tighter. 'I'm here for you, Athena, just as you were for me. I promise you will feel better once you let go of it, stop it dictating who you are, who you can be.'

She frowned at his words, aware there was a deeper meaning, a hidden message, but she was so lost in the pain of her memories that her mind couldn't work it out. She searched his face, looking into the depths of his dark eyes, seeking hints.

'What happened?' His whisper made her jump.

'I couldn't do anything.' As she spoke, she became the wide-eyed ten-year-old who'd kept calling out to her mother, asking her if she was okay. In between contractions her mother had seemed less panicky, less afraid, but as the contractions had increased in intensity and frequency, she'd become almost delirious with pain.

'You were a child.'

'But I should have been able to help her.' The agony in her voice shocked her and she bit down hard on her lip, but the story insisted on coming out. 'I called Father on the phone. And the emergency services, but she wouldn't let my hand go ...'

She shook her head at the utter helplessness she'd felt

that night as her mother, dripping in sweat, had collapsed into an exhausted heap on the floor, thankful when Alexio had guided her away as their father had taken over.

Kostas let her hand go and wrapped his arm around her, drawing her against him as he slid toward her. She let him enfold her in his embrace, the sanctuary his arms offered.

'I know how you feel.' He pressed his lips against her forehead and a small defiant bubble of laughter threatened to surface. Was that his sympathy kiss?

The strange urge to laugh subsided as quickly as it had come. 'I watched my mother, unable to help her – and later she died. It's my fault.'

There, she'd said it. Nobody, not even the emergency services and especially not her father, knew she blamed herself.

'You have no idea what that is like.' A sob wracked through her as he shushed her, stroking her hair gently with a reassuring rhythm.

Kostas nodded as his hand slid down the silky softness of Athena's hair. He knew exactly what that felt like, but whereas Athena had been a child, he'd been an adolescent, a boy on the verge of manhood. As his mother had drawn her last breath, he'd grown up. Become a cold hard man. Seeing his mother die had done that to him, along with all the anger he carried towards his father.

'I do.'

She pulled away from him, forcing him to stop the movements he'd been making without thinking. Holding her, kissing her forehead, reassuring her with gentle strokes to her hair had seemed the most normal and natural thing to do.

She blinked rapidly as she looked at him, her full lips seeming more pronounced against her pale face. 'How?'

'We have much more in common than either of us ever knew.' He leant his head to one side as he looked at her, a sad smile sliding to his lips. 'But I was seventeen. A young man when my mother died. And I was with her.'

'You couldn't do anything either?' she asked tentatively.

He shook his head. 'Nobody would have been able to. My mother's body couldn't cope with the alcohol. It gave up on her.'

'And you were there when she died?' she asked, as if she needed to hear it again, needed to make sure he was telling the truth. And for once in his life, he was. The whole truth. Just as she was.

Her pain, her fear, was bringing barriers crashing down. Barriers he'd had no idea she'd put up. Barriers he'd erected around himself too. But not every barrier. He'd never bring down the one he'd locked his heart behind when she she'd walked out on him. That one would remain firmly in place.

'I was.' He reached out and stroked her face. 'And it wasn't my fault, just as it wasn't your fault.'

She closed her eyes and leant into his caress, firing the heat back up. Heat that such a short time ago had nearly consumed them, nearly taken them to the point of lust. Because that was all it ever could be now. Athena had already made it clear that her love had been killed off, that this attraction, this desire, which was raging higher each minute they spent together, was nothing more than lust.

She'd just told him a heart-rending story from her childhood but still that desire burned in him. He looked into her eyes and saw it shining back at him. The kiss she'd brushed over his lips earlier had been induced from her sympathy for his story, his painful past, as much as from the spark of desire which was gaining strength all the time.

He didn't deserve to have even been loved by her, let alone married to her. He was an interloper in her world. A man who came from nothing but bad beginnings. And now she knew that.

Now he knew she wouldn't be able to give him what he wanted. He wasn't callous enough to force her to have his child. Even as he'd made his demand at his villa in Crete, he'd known he'd never push her to do that. That no matter what façade he presented to the world, he was not totally heartless. Not without some compassion.

As he'd made that outrageous demand, he'd hoped the passion they'd once had would make her consider his terms seriously. Clearly, she had. And it was destroying her.

'Kostas,' she whispered softly, big brown eyes slowly filling with heavy desire, looking into his.

He swallowed hard. He might well be a man who'd come from nothing, a man who'd married this beautiful woman, but he was a man of honour and values. Hot need was nudging at him again too, but he wasn't going to act on it.

Not tonight. Not after they'd shared so much of themselves.

'We should get some sleep,' he said quietly, brushing his fingers down her cheek again, instantly wishing he hadn't as she sighed seductively. 'We have a disbelieving Sebastianos to visit tomorrow and I still think our reconciliation should be played out publicly before the party.'

She drew in a breath, regret in her expression. 'You're right.' Then a small laugh slipped from her, but this time not like the hysterical one he'd thought was going to explode from her as she'd told him about the night her mother had died.

'I'm always right,' he said, not without a hint of seriousness as he stood up. 'I'll say goodnight.' He turned towards the guest room.

She shook her head. 'No. I want you to stay with me. To hold me.' The imploring look in her eyes took his breath away. It was all he'd wanted too. Such a short time ago he'd been filled with the need to have sex with her, to reclaim her in the most intimate way.

He was a hot-blooded male and he'd always used sex as his way of showing her that he loved her. But this connection, this awakening which was drawing him to her, was different. He craved closeness and intimacy, not sex and passion.

'Then I will hold you until you sleep.' He looked into her eyes and that sensation tugged at his heart again, threatening to blow open the door he'd locked love behind, and he knew that despite the fire of passion which had almost claimed them in a frenzy, he could lie in bed with her and hold her without making it sexual.

Tonight, wasn't the night for sex or lust. Tonight, was a time to be brave and allow the echo of the love they'd once shared to curl around them. To heal them.

Tomorrow he would re-erect the barriers, revert to the hard and callous man she'd accused him of being after he'd stated his terms to their deal.

He had to be that – or risk the pain of rejection again. Every person who'd ever meant something to him had left him or rejected him. Athena had done both. But she was his wife and he owed her his support. His strength.

He wanted to love her. If only things had been different.

'Hold me all night,' she said with a soft smile, dragging his mind from the turmoil it was in.

'If that's what you want.'

'It is.'

'Then I will,' Kostas said as he stood up and looked down at her. 'Go to bed and I will join you in a moment.'

She stood up and looked at him, sadness filling her eyes. 'Don't let me be alone tonight.'

He shook his head slowly, a smile on his lips. 'I won't. I promise.'

He watched her go and then poured himself another brandy, swigging it down in one go. As he placed the glass down, he heard her moving around in the bedroom and questioned if he could really do this.

You can – because you have hardened your heart.

The answer barged into him, making him stare at his reflection in the large mirror which took up most of the wall space opposite the windows. Beyond his image, the lights of distant Athens twinkled and far beyond that, the darkness of the sea met the night sky.

Damn it, she'd hardened it. Athena's mistrust and rejection.

Ever since that first day he'd seen her, all those years

ago, he'd loved her. He'd fought to make himself worthy of her, fought like hell and he'd done that. Financially at least. Had she ever loved him?

The question bounced off the mirror, slamming back into him.

The image of Sebastianos suddenly obliterated everything. The words the old man had rasped at him replayed in his mind again. *Go and make it right, Kostas. For Athena – and for me. You owe me that.*

Damn it. He needed to fight for Athena and for himself, the man he was beneath the exterior of success he'd portrayed to the world. That was what Sebastianos had challenged him to do as he'd glared up at him, demanding he make it right.

Kostas smiled. If he fought for her, made her realise they could be more than just lust, there might be a chance she'd one day see who he really was, despite all his revelations, and where he'd come from.

'Kostas.' Her whispered voice jolted him from his thoughts.

He turned to see her stood in the doorway, wearing a tee-shirt nightdress that only added to her air of vulnerability. Turning out the lights of the living room he walked towards the bedroom – to spend the night with his wife.

Athena pulled back the covers and got into bed, watching Kostas as he closed the bedroom door. With only the bedside lamp lighting the room, it was difficult to see his face, to read what he was thinking. But then she'd never really been able to do that. Kostas had always been like a closed book to her, only allowing her to view the pages he wanted her to see.

Since she'd arrived in Crete, she'd seen so many more of those pages. A flutter of hope filled her heart. Whatever it was that had pushed them apart, even as the passion had consumed them in the early days of their marriage, it was a barrier that was now slowly lowering. Something had shifted, changed. They'd opened up and shown their true selves in a way they'd never done before. Hope that he still had feelings for her surged forwards. Was it possible he was also hiding behind the show of only feeling lust?

He went into the bathroom and she lay down in the big bed. It was a routine they'd done so many times before they made love. But tonight, she didn't want anything more than to be held. She wanted to be in the safety of her husband's arms.

Yesterday morning he'd held her, wrapped her in his embrace when she'd nearly stumbled into the pool. Last night he'd comforted her and held her firmly against him. She'd felt safe. Just as she had at the poolside. Even then, she realised with a startle of shock, that was why she hadn't avoided his arms, hadn't moved away.

Even as she was preparing to tell him she wanted nothing from him other than to accompany her to Athens and see her father, she'd wanted him. Wanted what they'd shared as lovers and newlyweds.

She closed her eyes, sighing with regret, allowing the softness of the mattress and covers to soothe her, but it was Kostas's arms around her, his body warm against hers that would really do that.

She smiled as he climbed into bed with her, wearing

boxer shorts. Something he'd never done before. He was respecting her request – respecting her and that meant so much. Gently, he drew her into his arms as if he'd done the same thing every night for the last nine months. There wasn't a trace of awkwardness.

She moved against his chest, snuggling into his embrace, and inhaling the scent that had haunted her dreams almost every night she'd slept alone. He drew her closer and she lay still and content in his arms.

'You know I'd never allow anything bad to happen to you,' he whispered softly into her hair and she opened her eyes, her lashes blinking against his chest. He laughed softly. 'I know you are doing that evasive blinking thing with your eyelashes. I can feel them on my skin.'

'Sorry,' she said, making a concerted effort to stop it, but when she was unsure, it was either that or bite her lower lip.

'Don't be sorry,' he said softly, and she could feel his breath in her hair. 'I was teasing.'

He'd teased her only a short time ago, but in a totally different way, and it had been amazing.

'I would be with you every step of the way,' he said softly and she could feel him stiffen, feel his arms tense and she knew instinctively what he was referring to.

Their deal.

The baby she'd agreed to provide him with.

'You still want me to be the mother of your child, despite everything I've just told you?'

'I still want a child, yes.' The word was firm and decisive, and she moved back in the bed and looked up into his face. The soft light cast shadows over it, highlighting his cheekbones, making him look severe. 'With you, my wife.'

'How can I have your baby?' She could feel the hysteria brewing inside her again.

'If I look after you, be with you for everything.'

'Why is it so important?' she asked as a lump in her throat almost stole the question away.

'Doesn't every man want his own flesh and blood to inherit all he's strived for in life?'

She searched his eyes, her heart thumping hard against her ribs, her breathing short and fast.

'You and Father are of the same cloth,' she said, disappointment sliding over her. She'd thought Kostas didn't have the old-fashioned values her father insisted on upholding. But she'd been wrong. To her father she was only his daughter. To Kostas she was simply his wife. To both of them, the woman to bear children. Heirs.

He narrowed his eyes at her. 'I owe your father very much, but I am not the same man as he is.'

'Are you saying you don't crave the ever-needed male heir for your dynasty?'

For a moment she thought he was going to avoid answering as he'd done before. 'It would be good to hand everything over to my son, but I'd also do the same to my daughter – if I had one.'

'Then maybe you are not as quite the same as my father.' She couldn't help the smile that slipped to her lips, glad they'd gone off course, away from her having his child, to talking generally about him and her father. But did he really mean that?

'Not quite the same?' he teased, and she sensed he was as grateful to be off the subject of a baby as he was.

'In some ways you are the same, but different in others.' She whispered the words, relaxing into this new path in the conversation.

'And what makes us different?'

'My father hasn't forgiven Alexio for losing his life in that accident,' Athena whispered as annoyance slipped through her. If Alexio hadn't been driving so recklessly, was still here, she'd have been able to get to the bottom of why he'd set Kostas up. But now she knew why. He'd wanted to destroy her marriage because of intense jealousy. But the other issue, the bigger and far more terrifying issue would still have been there.

'It must be hard to lose a child,' Kostas said and she wondered if he was thinking of his father. Questioning how he could walk away.

'He lost his heir when he lost Alexio.' She saw Kostas's lips press firmly together in disapproval and hated the truth of those words. 'I think that is one of the reasons he is so insistent that we try and mend our marriage, so that he doesn't lose you. He looks upon you as a son. And now an heir. Another way you are the same.'

'How?' Kostas's hold on her felt tighter. More intense.

Her voice dropped to a whisper. 'He doesn't believe in divorce.' She pulled herself back to him, not wanting to talk any more this evening. They'd done enough, shared enough, for one night. 'Let's leave that conversation until tomorrow. Just hold me, Kostas.'

He inhaled deeply and held her even tighter. 'Sleep,' he said as he pressed his lips to her head. 'We can talk tomorrow.'

CHAPTER NINE

MEMORIES of the night he'd held Athena so close carried Kostas through the next few days. And like a gallant knight of old, each evening he'd retired to his own room. Athena seemed mellowed by his actions, wanting to spend more and more time with him. Although he'd had to prise her away from her work each day to visit Sebastianos before eating out to lay the foundations for their reunion.

Without any verbal agreement they'd reached a tentative truce, but he wanted their reunion to be real. He wanted an heir to fulfil the vow he'd made after Elias had needlessly died and for that he needed to be reconciled with his wife. At first it had been a convenient deal, but now he wanted more than a façade they were creating. But it could never be more if they both continued to hide behind excuses and work.

As they approached her father's hospital room, Kostas knew he had the power to make things right for her. Concern filled him as he sensed her tension building with each step and he took her hand, gently bringing her to a stop.

'What is it?' she asked, her eyes wide and full of question as she looked up at him.

He would do anything for her. He knew, as he looked into her brown eyes, that would always be the case. She was the only woman he'd loved.

'Kostas?' This time he could hear the panic in her voice and the question. 'What if Father doesn't get well? What if I can't give him all he wants?'

'Don't think like that,' he said, hearing again her pain as she'd told him that her father didn't consider her his heir. He would make the old man see she was far more capable than Alexio had ever been of taking the helm of the Petrakis empire. And more importantly, more willing than he was. He hated that she felt she needed to prove her worth to her father and that was something he was determined to make the old man see. 'Your father has something he needs to fight for, and I will make sure he does just that.'

'It's you he wants,' Athena said. 'You he wants to fight for which is why he must believe we are back together. He must see us as a couple.'

'He will.' Kostas stroked the softness of Athena's hair, this morning worn lose and straight. It gleamed with vitality and she looked so beautiful. But still that air of vulnerability clung to her in a way he'd never seen before.

'You'd do that? For me?' she whispered as her hand reached for the handle of her father's room.

He looked into her eyes and guilt pummelled him, like giant hailstones from an angry sky. He should never have ignored her for so long. Sebastianos was right. He should fight for her and he should have done it months ago – nine months ago. He'd just been too proud – and stubborn.

'I have to do something first.'

Athena frowned. 'What.'

'Kiss you.'

'Oh.' Her eyes widened and the surprise in them sparkled with happiness. He wanted to kiss her right now and begin the fight for her. As her lips lifted into a smile, he knew she wanted that kiss. He could sense the anticipation in her body. Feel her acceptance. Her need. It had been building since that night she'd slept entwined in his arms – and he couldn't ignore it any longer.

But he had to hear it from her.

He stepped close to her, the scent of perfume weaving into him. A scent he'd never forgotten and had carried with him every day since she'd walked away from him. The scent of the woman he'd loved with totally consuming passion.

His finger caressed lightly under her chin and she tilted it, looking up at him; her lips parted and the happy sparkle in her eyes was swamped with the far deeper swirl of desire.

'Your father told me to fight for you.' His thumb lingered lightly at the side of her chin and his finger stroked softly back and forth under her chin. 'And I will. Starting with a kiss.'

'You want to fight for me?' The question was a soft whisper and Kostas was mesmerised. He wanted to move his lips against her, to kiss awake the woman he'd fallen in love with.

'You and our marriage.' His voice was hoarse with the

intensity of the moment that was being played out in such starkly clinical surroundings. Maybe it was the best place. Nothing but white walls and ceilings, shiny floors, and that fierce sense that nothing bad could thrive there.

She leaned a little closer and he felt her breath on his face. 'Because of our deal,' she hesitated, her habit of biting at her lower lip getting the better of her. 'Or...' she hesitated. 'For real?'

To hell with the deal, Kostas wanted to rage. What he was feeling right now had nothing to do with their damn deal, but if he said that, if he told her how he felt, that he wanted her back in his life, wanted to genuinely try again at their marriage, she'd run. Again.

'Both,' he said softly, not wanting to alarm her. Not wanting to give himself away.

Her lashes lowered as she looked down, forcing him to move his hand away, and he thought he'd blown it, but when she looked back up at him there was that smile again.

'Then kiss me, Kostas.' Her command was strong even though her voice was still a whisper.

As she lifted her chin, moved closer to him, he wrapped his arms around her, wanting to kiss her hard. She splayed her palms on his chest and her eyes closed as his mouth hovered close to hers. She moved a little closer, bringing her body fully against his.

He closed his eyes as she responded and he strengthened the kiss, allowing all the desire he'd kept under restraint to be unleashed. Her hands slid up, around the back of his neck and her fingers moved into his hair.

She sighed softly, deepening the kiss.

His body was thrumming. Filled with passion and

desire. It felt like the sun had suddenly come out from behind dark clouds, as if he and the woman in his arms were bathed in a brilliant glow of warmth.

His tongue slipped into her mouth and as she responded, hers wrapping round his, a groan of contentment sliding from him into her.

'That's more like it.'

Sebastianos's brusque voice and laughter shattered the moment and Athena drew away hastily. He opened his eyes to see that the door to Sebastianos's room had been opened and a nurse stood waiting to come out. The brilliant glow he'd felt had been the sun pouring in through his window.

Or had it?

He looked at Athena, who laughed softly, mischievously, stepping back to allow the nurse to leave. Athena's lips were pink and plump. Evidence of his kiss. Her eyes danced with something, but he wasn't sure what.

Kostas held out his hand to her and with a wide smile she took it and they went into the room, together. For the first time since she'd told him what she wanted, he felt they were really together. Hope for their future infused every part of his body.

'Sebastianos,' Kostas greeted the old man who'd sat up and forwards, as if a new kind of energy filled him.

'How are you feeling today?' Athena's voice sounded different as she kept her hand in his and moved towards her father, drawing Kostas closer. Drawing him in to be part of them.

He nodded. His mouth pressed into a thoughtful

pout. 'Now I feel alive. I can see the beginnings of something to fight for.'

'Do you?' She laughed softly and looked up at Kostas, and his heart flipped over. For a second it was just them, alone and looking into each other's eyes. Echoes of the love he'd felt for her poured into him.

'Of course I do, I have my heir back.'

'Your heir?' Kostas turned his attention to Sebastianos, all the softness that kiss had made him feel gone, as he scowled at the old man. This was what Athena had told him and he'd found it almost impossible to believe. The old man adored his daughter, but now he could see that was all Sebastianos thought of her as. Just as Athena had said.

Sebastianos didn't consider his daughter to be his heir. He considered his son-in-law – him – as his heir. That was why he'd demanded Athena come to Crete to bring him back to Athens. He'd forced him to fight for Athena when all along it was the old man fighting for him.

Damn it. And he'd forced her to sacrifice herself, to accept the terms he'd put on their deal because of his own agenda with his past. And all she'd wanted was to make her father happy.

'You. At least until your marriage is blessed with a son.' Sebastianos pointed a finger, looking more like he was in a board meeting than a hospital bed. He'd certainly found his will to challenge.

But so had Kostas. Anger obliterated everything he'd felt as he'd kissed Athena.

He drew her close. 'This is your heir.'

Sebastianos glared at him. He'd never been challenged. He'd always been so powerful, so in charge. But not this time.

Athena remained in his embrace, her body tense and rigid and he knew she was looking at her father, then back to him. This wasn't what he was meant to be doing. He was supposed to be creating the illusion of a couple in love.

Instead he was opening up a battleground – with a man he'd never fought with before, a man he looked up to as a father-figure.

But this was worth fighting for. So was Athena. That thought lingered tantalisingly in his mind. Had Sebastianos intended this?

'My daughter?' Sebastianos said, eyes wide. He'd seriously never considered Athena could be his heir.

'Yes, your daughter,' Kostas snapped back at the old man, vaguely aware of Athena talking, saying his name, warning him to stop. But he couldn't. 'Your beautiful, but very capable daughter. She is your heir.'

'She is my daughter. I want a male heir and now that Alexio is gone, I want it to be you.'

Kostas laughed suddenly, sharply. Then he fixed Sebastianos with a firm glare. 'Drag yourself into the twenty-first century, old man.' He couldn't keep the challenge from his voice, and he heard Athena gasp, but he couldn't stop now. As far as he was concerned, this was the battle he needed to have – for her. 'She is your heir, your only heir and whilst I will help her in anything she needs, be at her side, she is far more capable of running your empire than you've ever given her credit for.'

'What are you saying?' Sebastianos demanded.

Kostas stood a little taller. 'That I will never accept

anything from you. Everything you wanted to hand over to Alexio is Athena's. I want nothing from you.' *Except Athena.*

He was shaking with rage, with the passion of his defence for the woman he'd married and once loved. He watched as Sebastianos sat back against his pillows, saying nothing. But the old man nodded.

He'd fought for Athena. His marriage.

'You two are unbelievable.' Athena was staggered at what she'd just witnessed. She and Kostas were supposed to be creating the illusion of a couple in love. She looked at her father. 'Are you alright?'

His gaze snapped from Kostas and the stand-off was broken. She sighed quickly and heavily, annoyed at Kostas for doing that, for challenging her father so harshly.

He did it for you. He fought for you, for what you want.

She ignored that thought as she looked at her father, wondering if she should call the nurse back. 'Father, are you okay? Do you need anything?'

She slipped from Kostas's embrace and perched on the edge of her father's bed, looking at him, feeling the panic rise as his eyes seemed glazed, as if he were far away.

She placed her hand over his. 'Father.' This time her voice was more insistent. He blinked and looked at her, studying her face as if seeing her for the first time.

Finally, her father spoke. 'He's right. I am a dinosaur.'

She shook her head slowly. 'No, you're not. At least, I don't think you are.'

He put his other hand over hers and she looked at hers between his. He'd given her so much since he'd been left to bring her up alone, but she'd never felt this much affection. As if he had been scared to love her. Scared of losing her like he'd lost his wife and baby daughter.

Bit by bit, things were making sense. The pieces of a jigsaw were being spread out in the order they needed to go into the puzzle. An order that made sense. All that was left for her to do, was slot each piece together. To complete the picture.

Her father looked beyond her, to Kostas, and she felt him move closer. Every nerve in her body was highly tuned to him after that kiss. The pleasure of it still lingering, despite the confrontation between the two men she loved.

Kostas placed his hand gently on her shoulder, his touch warm and reassuring. He was uniting them, bringing them together as a whole. It was what she wanted more than anything in the world. Her father happy and Kostas back with her – because she loved him.

She closed her eyes against that revelation, then slowly opened them again as her father patted her hand.

She'd never stopped loving Kostas.

She'd run because she was scared. Because she knew she couldn't create the next link in the chain, the next generation Kostas wanted. Not when she was the link that was so disjointed, and so out of line.

She was still scared, but whilst her father might be being honest, Kostas wasn't. He'd told her he would do all he could to make her father happy, to help him find the will to survive. He'd given her false hope because he still wanted his terms met. He'd even tried to convince her he'd be there with her if she had his baby.

She watched her father as he looked up at Kostas, nodding slowly, as if replaying their confrontation, agreeing with its outcome. 'You are right, Kostas.' He looked back at her. 'You are my only daughter, my surviving child and...' he paused as if to make sure he really wanted to say it. 'You are my heir.'

'Father,' she whispered over the lump in her throat. It sounded like he'd given up altogether. 'Not like this, please,' she said in a rush. 'It sounds like you are giving up, putting your affairs in order.'

'I am putting things in order. The right order. But I am not giving up. I intend to be around when you and Kostas have your children.' Her father smiled brightly. His eyes sparkled with the kind of vitality she hadn't seen in them for a long time. The kind that would help him claw his way back to health.

She blinked back the shock and felt Kostas's hand tighten on her shoulder.

'That's in the future,' she said carefully, wanting to keep her father's hope alive but not commit herself to doing the one thing she really couldn't do.

He laughed softly. 'Don't leave it too long, Athena – for my sake.'

'I won't.' She smiled even though the pressure was being pushed on her from more than one side. She was to inherit the business. A pang of sadness caught her unawares as she wished she could tell Alexio. He had all but destroyed her marriage, but he was still her brother and would always have a place in her heart.

'I'm serious,' her father jested, and she pushed all that

to one side – for now at least. Her father believed in them and he was happy, as if he had everyone he wanted, back around him.

'You'd better get yourselves to Phoebe's party.' He looked tired, the energy their discussion had taken was almost too much and a tinge of worry crept back.

'We will see you tomorrow.' Kostas spoke, startling her.

Her father shook his head. 'Take some time together, make up for those months apart.' Then he laughed. 'I'm not sure the nurses will tolerate another display of passion, so you'd better stay away until you've got that under control.'

* * *

Her father's words had still been ringing in her ears as she and Kostas returned to the villa. She was torn between elation that he believed them, that he was happy and prepared to acknowledge her as his heir. But that didn't detract from the mounting fear that he too now expected her to have a baby.

'Thank you,' she said as she joined Kostas on the terrace, the sound of cicadas filling the heat of the afternoon.

He turned to look at her. His expression softer than usual, as if he'd been lost in thoughts of his own, thoughts that had dropped his guard.

'I'm sorry I got forceful with your father.'

'Don't be.' She moved to him, placing her hand on his arm. Her emotions were scattered like autumn leaves in the wind. He was acting like he cared – loved her. But his terms were still between them. Was that why he'd insisted she didn't work so hard this week? Was he trying to ensure he got what he wanted out of this enforced reconciliation?

'I shouldn't have been so hard on him.' Kostas's voice was fierce, and that unguarded moment was gone.

'Until I heard you saying those words to my father – fighting for me – I hadn't allowed myself to remember the pain of knowing I could never be what he wanted, no matter how hard I tried, but...'

She wanted to move past her father's rejection. But new doubts lingered. Was everything Kostas had said and done this afternoon part of the illusion of being in love? Was her father really prepared to accept her as his heir? She bit her lip against the pain of those questions. Since the night her mother had died, she'd held on to so much pain, adding to it all the time. Could she really let it all go?

Kostas turned to her, brushing her hair from her face, the softness in his eyes making her heart flutter. It been in his eyes at the hospital. Before he'd kissed her.

A kiss that had felt so real, she'd almost believed it was. Almost. Because even though she'd hoped the words he'd spoken to her father hadn't been part of their charade of togetherness, that kiss had definitely been a smokescreen. It was almost as if he'd known that at any minute a nurse would open the door and that her father would see for himself the raw passion even she couldn't deny was there.

But raw passion was lust, and lust wasn't love. Her heart hammered as those thoughts careered around her head. And she was in love with Kostas. And if you were in love with someone, didn't you want to do all you could to make them happy? Give them what they wanted?

'I told him the truth. You are his rightful heir and so very capable of running his business – without a man at your side. But it's more than that, isn't it?'

The heat of the afternoon bore down on them and Athena felt like she'd come to a fork in the road of her life. She could choose honesty or denial.

'Yes,' she whispered, choosing honesty with barely any hesitation. 'I never wanted for anything after Mother died, I knew he loved me but after that night he found it hard to show. Today, I saw his love for me and it's you who took him to that point.'

She couldn't tell him she still feared a repeat of all she'd gone through if she was ever brave enough to have a baby then had a little girl. She didn't want to break this soft spell by mentioning their deal. That conversation could wait.

'Athena, beautiful Athena,' he whispered as he moved towards her, close enough to kiss her. 'You deserve so much love.'

She closed the gap between them, brushing her lips over his, feeling everything that had ever held her emotions back being pushed to the side. All she wanted was to give in to whatever it was between them – because she loved him.

She brushed her lips over his and whispered, 'Thank you.'

'Today has been a day of revelations,' he whispered as she looked up into his eyes, her heart pounding hard in her chest.

She slipped her arms around his neck, entwining her

fingers together, feeling his hair against them. Her breathing deep and hard as he wrapped his arms around her, drawing her even closer.

'Let's not talk anymore.' She brushed her lips over his, her heart singing with joy, her body alive with desire as he responded, slowly moving his lips beneath the demanding pressure of hers.

The intensity of the passion which filled his body took Kostas by surprise. Nothing would give him more pleasure than to whisk her off her feet and take her upstairs to finish what had been started so many times since last Saturday morning.

But he had his part of the deal to fully fulfil. He and Athena were expected at Phoebe's name day party this evening and after the long months apart, the tempting torture of having spent a night with her in his arms, not going to the party seemed very appealing. But when he did take her to bed, when he finally let loose the desire which hummed in the air now, weaving around them with more intensity than the heady scent of flowers on the terrace, he wanted to take it to its ultimate conclusion.

He wanted to make love to her.

He wanted to use his body to show her how right they were together.

Unable to help himself, his hand slid down her back, the lace of her dress against his palms as he cupped her bottom. A soft sigh slipped from her into his mouth as she touched her hips against his, and he pressed his eyes tightly shut as a spear of desire shot straight through him.

Lust, that was what she'd called it.

Love didn't do that. Love would be there all the time. Just as his had once been, despite being locked safely away in an attempt at self-preservation.

'Kostas,' Athena said, pushing his desire higher – his control lower, 'I want more than this. I want you.'

For a moment he hung on the edge of a mountain he'd never intended to be on, a mountain of control and denial. He wanted Athena, wanted to satisfy his burning need for her, right now.

He drew back, looking into her eyes, dark and swirling with desire. 'I want you too,'

Her eyes searched his face. 'But?'

He laughed softly, brushing her hair gently from her face. 'But?' he whispered, the intensity in the air around them increasing. 'We have a party to get ready for, not to mention the guests we need to convince that we are reunited.'

She blinked rapidly several times. 'Of course, the façade of being in love again.'

Was that a tinge of disappointment in her voice?

'It shouldn't be that hard to convince them. It was real once.'

He wanted it to be real again, but he'd buried his love behind a massive barrier of male pride, and he wasn't about to unleash that emotion.

Lust was safer. Far safer.

'Once,' she said bluntly, then looked up at him, her eyes telling him something different. As if claiming that, despite everything that had happened, they could become lovers again.

He wanted to kiss her like he had at the hospital, but

sense prevailed. 'We are still married, still man and wife, so of course it will be real.'

'Yes,' she said, thoughtfully, looking up at him. 'It can be as if we are falling in love again.'

'It can, *agape mou.*' Slowly he lowered his head and brushed her lips over hers as she moved hers beneath his without resistance.

'Do you really believe that?' The hesitancy in her voice nearly broke his heart and he hated that he'd made her feel like that. First her father and then him. They'd both made her feel afraid to love. Or be loved...

'Don't look at me like that,' he all but growled.

'Like what?' She smiled coyly, blatantly aware of the effect she was having on him.

'With all that passion and desire in your eyes.'

'Don't you want passion and desire?' she whispered, sending shockwaves around his body, pushing his control to the limit.

He brushed his palm down her hair again, so close he could kiss her. 'I do, and if we weren't due at a family party very soon, I'd take you to your room and unleash all that passion.'

'I want you to,' she whispered as she pressed her lips to his. 'Tonight.'

CHAPTER TEN

ATHENA'S BODY had been humming with anticipation all evening, making every hour of the party a hazy blur. Every time Kostas touched her hand, her arm, or whenever he looked at her, her heart had raced. The heady expectation of passion once they returned to the villa had rushed over her like a waterfall after a stormy downpour.

She knew giving in to it would complicate things between her and Kostas, but weren't they already complicated enough?

'Have I told you how beautiful you look this evening?' Kostas whispered in her ear as he leant closer, the fresh spice of his cologne invading her senses, ratcheting up her need to surrender to him, allow her love to show – one last time.

Athena laughed softly, holding her glass of champagne as if it were a lifeline to sanity. 'Several times.'

When she'd bought the full-length blush, pink dress adorned with tiny sequins, she'd never anticipated she'd be wearing it with her husband back at her side. His gaze flickered down to the low neckline and suddenly she felt very sexy in the spaghetti straps.

'Then I must say it again.' The husky tone of his voice sent a tremor of anticipation through her, making her breathe deeper, her breasts rising and falling beneath his hungry gaze.

'When you look at me like that,' she said, feeling shyness creep over her. 'I feel beautiful. Desired.'

He reached out, pushing her hair she'd allowed to revert to its natural curl, back from her shoulder. The touch of his finger on her shoulder was so intense, so powerful that she almost sank to the floor, her knees suddenly weakening.

'And you are. Beautiful and desired.' She looked up at him, her heart hammering even harder. His eyes swirled with passion and there would be no avoiding it now.

Tonight, she would be his. Totally and completely.

Tonight, she wanted to forget about deals and terms. She wanted to give herself up to the pleasure of being loved by the man she'd loved once with such abandon. The man she was still in love with. She wouldn't allow herself to acknowledge that for him it was lust. She'd cling to her ideal of love – for tonight at least.

'Then you are handsome and...' She paused, that shyness creeping over her, causing her lashes to flutter down. She looked back up, her eyes meeting his. It was as if the music and laughter of the party had been turned off. As if she and Kostas had been transported to a place where it was just them. She took in his strong body, resplendent in a tuxedo that hugged every strong muscle to perfection, shyness making her blush in a way she'd never done before. 'Sexy.'

Kostas moved closer, brushing his lips over hers so fleetingly yet so softly, a little gasp of pleasure slipped from her. He moved closer and whispered in her ear. 'You make me feel ...' She felt his breath against her ear as he paused. It was the most erotic sensation ever. 'Sexy.'

The pulse of desire between her legs became so intense she needed to move away from him. Away from the temptation of throwing herself into his arms and demanding he take her home right now and make love to her.

'Athena.' Her cousin's voice cut through the haze of passion and she watched, disappointment sliding through her as Kostas stepped back, allowing Phoebe to hug her. It should have broken the delicate threads that were re-joining her to Kostas and, looking quickly at him, she knew it hadn't. That sexy smile, the come-to-bed look of promise in his eyes, left her in no doubt. That the connection was merely on hold.

'It's a beautiful party, Phoebe, and you look stunning.'

Phoebe laughed. 'Not as much as you do. Being loved up again suits you.' She glanced cheekily at Kostas. 'Both of you.'

Athena blushed, suddenly aware that it was quite probable that every person at the party knew how much she wanted Kostas, sensed the power of the sexual attraction arcing between them.

She didn't know what to say. How to divert the attention.

Kostas placed his arm around Phoebe's shoulders.

'You are an incredibly beautiful woman and one day, a man will desire you in the way I desire Athena.'

He'd charmed Phoebe into a blushing meltdown and Athena smiled, knowing exactly how helpless against that charm her cousin would be feeling right now.

Phoebe laughed, turning to look at Kostas. 'You should take her home now.' She was laughing giddily. 'Give the family something to really talk about.'

'Maybe I will.' Kostas focused his full attention on Phoebe, and Athena knew the poor girl would be melting beneath the intensity of it. 'With your permission of course.'

Phoebe laughed coyly, placing her hand at her chest. 'Yes.' She looked at Athena and smiled warmly. 'Go. Now.'

'Then I will say goodnight.' Kostas took Phoebe's fingertips and lifted them to his lips, kissing them lightly. Poor girl. She didn't stand a chance against him.

Neither did she.

'She's right,' Kostas said as he moved closer to Athena again, watching Phoebe move on to mingle with other guests.

Athena was acutely aware of the scrutiny of those guests. Some covert and some open, but she and Kostas were certainly creating a buzz amongst her family members. She couldn't help questioning if the way Kostas made her feel was simply part of the façade of reunion. Was the charm and seduction he was lavishing on her this evening part of fulfilling her terms so that he could then demand his?

She shut the thought down.

Tonight, she didn't want to think.

Tonight, she wanted to feel every bit of raw desire between them. Because, even if nothing else was, that was honest and true.

His hand brushed against hers at her side and looking up at him, she slipped hers into his. The warmth of his hand as it wrapped around hers as reassuring as it was seductive. Unable to stop herself, she licked her lips in anticipation of his kisses. Hard, demanding, and bruising kisses. Kisses she'd be able to feel long after the passion tonight promised had subsided.

His attention flew to the small movement as she licked her lips and fireworks exploded in his eyes. This time, she knew there wouldn't be any stopping them. When he kissed her and took her in his arms, the passion and desire would reach full height and the ultimate conclusion. It was written in the dark swirling depths of his eyes.

'Take me home, Kostas.' Her voice had become husky and full of desire and the effect it had on him only intensified the burning need for him. She'd never felt so much feminine power. This strong, dominant male was completely under her command. Hers to control as she wished.

And she wished – very much.

Sitting next to Athena in the car as they had been driven through the streets of Athens, then out towards the hillside and her villa, had been excruciating. Kostas had wanted to draw her close, but he hadn't dared.

Not just because the passion would threaten to explode right there in the back of the car, but because of the love he wasn't ready to explore yet. That would be to risk her rejection again. No, he would not allow that emotion to take centre stage. He would focus on what she'd claimed to want – passion and lust.

'That seemed to take forever,' he said as the car finally pulled up in front of the villa. His entire body on alert to every move she made, every look she cast his way. Painfully alert.

She placed her hand on his arm and he realised he'd been clenching his hands into fists with the effort of not reaching for her and more importantly, controlling his emotions. 'And now we are alone.'

He looked down at her, the smoky make-up of her eyes highlighting the passion in them. The hunger for him. The throb of need for her intensified, making him feel the most powerful man alive.

'And do you want to be alone with me?' His question slipped out in a hoarse whisper as desire notched up ever higher.

She leaned across the car, the leather of the seats scrunching softly as she did so, and pressed her lips to his cheek, her breath soft on his face as she whispered her reply. 'So very much.'

'I want to reclaim you as my wife, Athena. I want our reunion to be real,' he whispered, resisting the urge to kiss her now, to demand so much more than soft sighs and light kisses. 'I want to make you mine once more. Completely and totally.'

'Kostas,' she sighed as she looked at him, her eyes a smouldering brown.

'I can't switch off how I feel about you.' His fingers stroked up and down her cheek and he fought against the urge to tell her that feeling was love, but he didn't want to startle her, didn't want her to withdraw from him. Or worse, his biggest fear – be rejected.

'I don't want you to,' she said so softly.

He brushed his lips, lingeringly, teasingly over hers. 'Then we should go inside where we can be truly alone.'

'Yes, we should,' she breathed against his lips and it took all his willpower to move away from her, to open the car door and get out into the sultry warm air of the night. The driver, he noticed, had stepped away from the car, keeping a discreet distance. The passion between Athena and himself must be so noticeable.

Without another word, he took her hand and entered the villa. At the bottom of the grand staircase she paused, her smile soft, with a hint of nerves. The backs of his fingers caressed her cheek and she leaned into the touch, closing her eyes.

When she opened them, they were dark and swirling with such desire he had to hold back the urge to kiss her and there on the stairs slip the sparkling gown from her shoulders and kiss her breasts.

'Take me to bed, Kostas,' she whispered as she moved closer to him, her hands sliding inside his jacket and palms pressing against his chest.

Athena slid her hands up towards the black bow tie that looked so sexy on Kostas and with her eyes locked with his, pulled it gently until it came undone. Mischief urged her on and she laughed softly, revelling in her power as he bit back a groan, his hands holding her at her waist as if he didn't dare move from them from there.

Just the way he looked at her made her feel sexy and powerful. In control. But there was something else in his eyes, something she'd seen before. He'd had that same heaviness in his eyes when he'd told her he loved her – before they'd shut each other out.

Hope grew from the flicker that had been trying hard to stay alight since she'd arrived in Athens with him. The flicker that had flared a little higher after he'd stood up to her father – for her. Was it possible...?

'This is what I've wanted since I saw you stood at the side of the pool.' Kostas's voice was hoarse, and it broke that dangerous trail of thought.

'Since then?' she asked boldly, taking control of her reckless emotions as well as the situation. She pulled the tie from beneath his shirt collar slowly, then held it out at her side, raising her eyebrows suggestively. She tossed the tie away and began to unfasten the buttons of his shirt.

Never in all the time they'd been together, had they teased one another so many times and not had sex. Her mind flew back to that moment he'd trailed his fingers so seductively down her body. This time, she would be in control. This time she wanted far more than that teasing torture.

His tanned chest, dusted with hairs, became visible as she opened his shirt. She moved closer, lowering her head to press her lips against his chest, feeling his grip on her waist intensifying.

She kissed upwards then stood up, to kiss his lips. He tried to kiss her back, but she moved away, keeping everything light and teasing, just as he'd done to her. With a flick of her eyebrows, she pushed her hands between his shirt and jacket, sliding it off his shoulders and moving away from him, forcing him to let her go. The jacket slid to the floor.

He looked so sexy her breath caught in her throat. His shirt opened to his waist and his eyes as black as the darkest night sky.

'Let's go upstairs,' she said, picking up the skirt of her dress in one hand and taking his in the other.

Kostas followed, one step behind her as they made their way up the wide staircase. At the top she turned and moved to him, pulling at his shirt, and freeing it from the black trousers which hugged his hips and long thighs to perfection.

His dark eyes fixed her to the spot as he undid his shirt cuffs, and pulled the soft white fabric from his body, dropping it to the floor. She ignored the urge to press her lips to his, to demand the deepest kiss possible, and trailed her fingers down his chest, following the dark line of his hair. He groaned, closing his eyes and she unfastened his trousers, pulling the zip down over the hardness of his erection. Hot throbs of excitement fired through her as her fingers skimmed over that hardness.

His eyes snapped open. 'I won't be able to wait if you touch me like that.' His jaw clenched in control and his chest moved in and out with the force of his hard breathing.

'Then maybe you should remove your trousers,' she teased, that surge of power, combined with her need for the man she'd married, making her bolder than she'd ever been.

He laughed, a low sexy sound, but obeyed her command. He kicked off his shoes and socks, then opened the zip on his trousers fully, the black fabric sliding down his strong legs.

She swallowed hard as he kicked them aside, standing in only black briefs which did nothing to hide his aroused hardness. With a wicked smile on his lips, he put his fingers on the waistband of the briefs and she knew he would take them off unless she stopped him. And she had to stop him because she was in charge.

'No,' she said, taking one hand away and leading him towards their suite, the trail of his clothes making her smile.

She led him through the sitting room he'd teased her so mercilessly in and towards her bedroom. She drew him to a stop beside the bed and looked at him, wanting to kiss him, wanting to feel his lips on hers, hard and demanding, but once she did...

'I think you are wearing more clothes than me.' His smile sent her pulse racing and she breathed deeply, her breath getting more ragged by the minute as the passion and tension grew. 'May I?'

She drew in a long breath. 'Yes.'

Much to her surprise, he knelt in front of her and lifted the hem of her dress. As his fingers caressed her ankle, her eyes closed with the heat of his touch. With swift deftness, he undid the strap of her sandal, lifting her foot, and taking it off. As she stood, slightly lower, he did the same to the other and Athena knew what would be next.

He stood up, a wicked gleam in his eyes as he towered over her, but she kept her chin lifted in defiance of the few inches she'd lost from taking off her heels. Then with both hands together, he reached out and hooked his finger under each of the fine spaghetti straps of her dress.

She closed her eyes as he moved them slowly off her shoulder then turned, so he could unfasten the zip at the back. His touch was gentle, and she turned slowly back to him, holding the dress to her breasts, opening her eyes. He watched her as she let go, her nipples hardened as the dress slid down, exposing her breasts.

'So beautiful,' he whispered as he pulled the sequined fabric lower, until it slithered down over her hips dropping to her feet, leaving her in nothing but the tiniest cream silk panties.

She reached for his briefs, almost locking her fingers into the waistband.

He caught her hand and slowly shook his head. 'It's still my turn.'

Then he slipped his fingers inside the top of her panties and gently pulled them down, going down to his knees as he did so. With his head bent, he lifted one foot, encouraging her to step out of them, then pulling the dress away, leaving her without a trace of clothing.

'Is it my turn yet?' she asked, feeling suddenly shy, but determined not to give in to it. He looked up at her and shook his head slowly again.

'Not quite.'

His finger began the same trail it had followed before, but this time, from her toe upwards. She shuddered with pleasure as she watched him, watching her. The trail moved up over her knee, up her thigh, she thought he'd begin it again on the other leg, but instead he knelt up in front of her, taking her thighs in each hand as he kissed the dark curls at the apex of her thighs.

She plunged her fingers into his hair as he kissed a little lower. The heat of his breath teasing her, making her long for his touch. She tilted her pelvis, her body begging him for that kiss and instead of teasing her as he'd done far too much already, his tongue touched and explored exactly where she needed it, making her gasp and grip his hair, pressing him closer to her.

She closed her eyes as the exquisite pleasure carried her towards the edge, where the stars would meet her and take her higher. 'Kostas,' she breathed his name as she clung to the last threads of control. She didn't want to go there yet, not without him. 'Not yet.'

He drew back and as her body shook with need, she opened her eyes and looked down at him. He watched her, waiting for her to come back from the brink of ecstasy he'd almost pushed her over.

'My turn,' she said as control slipped back over her. 'Stand up.'

Her command was firm, and his response slow and teasing. She took the waistband of his briefs, lifted the fabric away from the rigid hardness and then pulled them lower, copying his actions of moments ago. She knelt at his feet, trailing her fingers upwards over his hair-roughened legs, watching him all the time. Then she took him into her mouth, watching the pleasure wash over the controlled expression on his face as his fingers slid into her hair. His moan of pleasure so erotic her whole body ached for him.

'No more,' he gasped as he caught her face in his hands, forcing her to cease her torment. 'We are equal now.'

'We are,' she said as he drew her to her feet and she

knew that when it came, sex would be wild and explosive. All it needed was for one of them to let go of the rigid control they were both trying to hang on to.

He sat on the end of the bed and drew her to him. She straddled his legs as he kissed her stomach, then moved to her breasts, heavy and full of need for his caress, his kiss. Her hardened nipples ached with the need to feel his lips around them, and she gasped, throwing back her head when he took one in his mouth, nipping and licking it until her blood roared with the need for complete and utter satisfaction.

'Do you want me to use a condom?' He whispered the question against her breast and her heart filled with love. Even in the headiest passion, he cared enough to ask her, to remember all she'd told him about not wanting to ever be pregnant.

'I'm still on the pill.' She managed to gasp the words out as he turned his attention to her other breast.

'Then there is nothing to stop us,' he said, looking up at her, his voice deep and husky with desire.

She couldn't speak now. All she could do was shake her head.

He smiled and held her hips as she sat astride him and lowered herself onto his hardness. Explosive passion erupted, taking her further and higher than she'd ever been.

She tried to keep her control, but she couldn't hide anything from him anymore. This was what she wanted. He was what she wanted. The man she loved.

. . .

Kostas closed his eyes as Athena took him deep inside her. Every move she made was pure torturous pleasure. The wave of desire crashing over him the most intense he'd ever known and within seconds his body shook with the control of holding back.

Athena cried out as ecstasy caught hold of her, her face pressed into his shoulder as she rode him, snatching him up and taking him with her – past her – as the first waves of his orgasm gripped him, making him cry out.

Then she joined him, riding the wave of pleasure together, bodies clinging, gasps entwining in the silence of the room.

'Athena,' he growled out her name, biting back the words he wanted to say, forcing himself to think of the physical pleasure for them both. As the final wave snatched at him, he thrust himself in deeper and harder.

'I love you, Kostas,' she cried out as she clung to him, her orgasm taking her higher as she tensed around him.

His breathing was hard and fast as he held her tight against him, still buried deep within her. His heart hammered, his body hot against hers. The power of such explosive sex numbed his mind, making thought almost impossible.

Then the echo of her words descended around him like tiny pieces of shattered glass.

She'd always said that when she made love to him. Every time she climaxed, she always said that. Now he knew why he'd been so reluctant to take the step, to have sex with her – his wife.

Because he wouldn't know if she'd say it out of habit or if she'd mean it.

I love you, Kostas.

The words settled around him, quietening to a whisper. A whisper which haunted him.

As if sensing his reservation, she slid off him and lay on the bed, spent, and sated. Gloriously naked and forever tempting. She turned her head, her hair splaying out like silk around her as she looked at him, questions in her eyes. Questions he wasn't ready to answer.

He needed to cool off – literally.

'I'm going to take a shower,' he said. The wrench of his heart as her expression filled with hurt was so powerful and he leant over and kissed her softly on the lips. 'Then afterwards...' he teased as he trailed a finger down over her stomach.

She swallowed then smiled at him. 'Afterwards?'

He didn't know what would come after this. Right now, he needed to sort his feelings out. She'd said she loved him. He had loved her once. Still would do, if only he dared. It should be simple, but it wasn't. Far from it.

'We will resume,' he said, his mind racing in turmoil.

'Can't wait,' she said, propping herself up on her elbow as he stood up and headed for the bathroom and the ice-cold jets of the shower his body demanded and his mind needed.

As the water thundered on his head, he couldn't stop thinking. If love had brought them together again, how could he force her to remain his wife, knowing her worst fear was the one thing he wanted – needed – most. When he'd asked her if he needed a condom, it had unleashed that devil of doubt.

But if he loved her, wasn't it better to set her free, to end the marriage so that they could both have the happiness they deserved?

He wrapped a towel around his hips, taking another to dry his hair, looking at his reflection in the partially steamed mirror. There didn't seem to be another way. He could never force any woman to bear his child. The cold terms he'd made at his poolside had been out of anger that she'd turned up and ordered him to heel.

It was his rebellion.

Now it was his undoing.

He tossed the towel angrily into the bath. There was only one way to sort this. To keep his love for her hidden. To set the woman he loved free.

He opened the bathroom door, preparing himself to do just that but the sight that met his eyes, melted his heart. Athena was asleep. Naked and vulnerable, asleep on the bed. Hating himself for his weakness, his inability to tell her the truth, admit his feelings, he gently climbed onto the bed and took her in his arms, drawing her close and covering them both with the soft blanket.

One more night, he told himself as he inhaled the scent of the woman he'd always loved. *One more night*.

CHAPTER ELEVEN

ATHENA WOKE TO A DARKENED ROOM, covered in a soft blanket and with Kostas's arm around her. She felt safe. Protected. But did she feel loved?

In the darkness she could just make out the shapes of the bedroom furniture. Kostas's love was like those darkened shapes. It lingered beyond what she could immediately see. There but not quite. Not close enough to touch or feel, but there somewhere, hidden away.

Then she remembered the words she'd cried out as she'd reached an orgasm like no other. She'd left him in no doubt she loved him, saying those words, just like she'd always done when they'd made love, before her fear had got the better of her. Before she'd turned her back on him. On a future together.

His silence had been louder than her words, but she'd been so caught up in the ecstasy of the moment she hadn't immediately realised Kostas hadn't responded. A chill slid down her spine. She'd made a mistake, giving in to her feelings. Allowing her love to surface. She'd exposed the very part of her she'd needed to keep secret. Her heart.

She turned in his arms, suddenly aware of her nakedness. He was asleep, and although her movement disturbed him, it didn't wake him but his hold on her tightened. In the dimness of the room she could just make out his face and how relaxed it was. This was the completely unguarded version of Kostas. The Kostas she'd loved since she was a teenager. The man he rarely showed anyone, not even her.

Unable to help herself, she kissed him.

Kostas stirred and opened his eyes, looking at her. The unguarded version of her husband disappearing in an instant.

'I didn't want to wake you.' He spoke carefully, as if he was choosing every word he said with extreme caution.

'I wish you had.' She saw a fierce glitter enter his eyes that even the darkness couldn't hide. Something was wrong. She sat up, reached for the bedside light, and switched it on, blinking against its brightness. 'What's wrong, Kostas?'

He sighed and sat up. 'We are.'

She frowned, not able to understand what he was saying. Only a short time ago they'd been making love and she'd cried out just how much she loved him. But Kostas hadn't been making love. He'd been having sex. Her husband no longer loved her, and it had been her stupid fears that had killed his love for her.

'How are we wrong?' Her words jabbed from her, making her stomach turn over as if she were on a rollercoaster.

'We shouldn't be here like this, making deals to get what we want. Sealing it with sex.' He stood up and she noticed he'd put on his briefs. The image of him standing by the bed was almost a mirror image of the man stood by his pool on Saturday morning. The cold heartless man who had demanded she have his baby.

And now he was saying they shouldn't have slept together. Or had sex.

'That sex,' she said, putting emphasis on the word. 'Was not sealing any deal. Not as far as I'm concerned.'

'What was it then, Athena? Lust?' He threw her original explanation for the sizzling attraction back at her and she resisted the urge to hurl an agreement at him.

'Part of our fake reconciliation.' Pain seared into her heart. The heart that had just opened to him, let him back in because for some reason she'd thought he'd be there for her. The fight he'd made for her with her father, made her feel sure he wouldn't push her aside and take all she'd worked for. But there was still his demand for a child. Would he really insist she see it through after all she'd told him?

He glared angrily at her. 'And who is here to witness this part?'

'We are.' She dragged the blanket around her, her nakedness making her feel far too exposed, emotionally as well as physically. 'By giving in to the lust, we've made it very real. Everyone at the party must have thought we couldn't keep our hands off one another. Phoebe did.'

'And everything you've done has been with the sole aim of achieving that?' His question rushed at her, catching her off guard, making her feel even more vulnerable.

'Yes.' She lifted her chin defiantly. She wasn't going to let him know how much her heart was breaking.

'And everything you've said, too?'

She paused for a moment, her heart thudding. 'Everything.'

He drew in a sharp breath. 'Then it would seem you have all you wanted. Your father has found the will to fight and he now considers you his heir.'

But that wasn't everything she wanted. Far from it.

'I am grateful for your support in that. It is, may I remind you, something you did without being asked to do so.'

Kostas shook his head as if he couldn't believe what she was saying. She couldn't believe it either. 'I fought for you, Athena. I fought because ...' The uncharacteristically passionate outburst trailed off. He dragged his hands through his hair, turning to pace across the room, towards the more dimly lit corner.

Because of what? She held her breath.

'We shouldn't have had sex.' He said it again, as if he wanted to rub it in, make sure she knew they hadn't made love. 'It's just made everything a complicated mess.'

'But the expectation of it certainly made for a convincing act of reconciliation,' she retaliated, hurt and pain cutting through her, making her body feel like ice, her words like shards of glass.

She stood up, no longer caring she was naked, and retrieved her dressing gown from the wardrobe, as putting it on and tying the belt tightly she turned to look at Kostas.

As soon as she did, she could feel the anger radiating from him. If anger was what he wanted, then she had more than enough to match his. Her anger was born out of disappointment and humiliation.

Rejection.

Inwardly she groaned. How could she have been so stupid to think, even for a minute, that he still felt something for her, that he was falling in love with her all over again? Every time he'd lulled her into that false sense of security, it had been as part of his act. He'd been meeting his terms of their deal.

She turned from him, not wanting to feel those waves of anger, and sat in the chair in the corner of the bedroom. A corner where the glow of the bedside lamp didn't reach. A place she felt safe to lick her wounds.

'Acting is all this has ever been about.' His voice was short and sharp as he strode back across the bedroom, away from her, his hands ploughing through his hair again.

She looked away from him, her attention now on the Stefana crowns she and Kostas had worn on their wedding day. The crowns which had been placed on their heads by the priest, then intertwined by the Koumbaros three times to symbolise unity. An old wedding tradition, but it hadn't helped them. Now the delicate white bands, joined with a ribbon, seemed to be mocking her from the glass case she'd kept them in.

She looked back to Kostas as he turned to face her. She'd gone to Crete to ask Kostas to see her father. To ask him if he'd act the part of being back together with her for her father's sake, but really, she'd used her father's illness. She'd wanted Kostas back in her life. She just hadn't been able to tell him because that would mean admitting she'd used all that Alexio had done as a cover to walk away. She'd been terrified by Kostas's first tentative mention of having a family. And equally as terrified that he would take everything from her. Running had been easier.

'It wasn't even about your father, was it, Athena?' His angry question fired at her.

She shook her head and looked down to her lap, misery filling her. If only she could speak to him, tell him the real reason. That her fear of losing everything had driven her from the marriage. Just as it had kept her from mending it.

Her heart began to thump as realisation hit her. Her love for Kostas, the love she'd tried to hide since she'd walked away from him nine months ago, was stronger than ever. When he'd fought for her, stood up to her father, she'd believed he would be on her side, helping her through anything – from pregnancy, to taking over from her father when the time came.

Inwardly she groaned with the agony. She hadn't been prepared to even consider having his baby, despite the fact that being a mother was the one thing she'd secretly yearned for. As Kostas fought her corner, stood up to her father, she'd known she wanted to give him the one thing that was so important to him. Because despite her fear of pregnancy, it was what she wanted too – if he was there for her.

Kostas plunged his hands through his hair as frustration fired through him. He wanted to feel pain, anything to stop the agony of knowing Athena didn't love him.

He was merely part of a bigger plan. A plan that

didn't involve him – unless she agreed to his terms and became the mother of his child.

He looked at her, sitting in the darkest corner of the room, and everything he'd felt last night as he'd asked her if he needed a condom flooded back. Then he'd been consumed and driven by desire, but he'd still made sure he looked after her, prevented a pregnancy she didn't ever want – was afraid of.

His rubbed his hands down his face, drawing in a deep breath, then let them fall to his side, all the fight, all the anger slipping away as if the sun were rising over the Acropolis, bathing it in a soft warm glow.

He loved Athena. And she didn't love him.

He wanted to be a father. She didn't want to be a mother.

He and Elias had wanted to create business empires, have marriages that would last forever and fill their lives with children. They'd both been driven by the need to create the kind of family they'd never known.

Since that terrible night when he'd found Elias's beaten body on the road, Kostas had been consumed by the need to do all that in memory of his friend – for his friend. And he'd thought Athena was the woman to do that with. Now he had to accept he was wrong.

'It was about Father,' she said softly from the darkened corner of the room, and he could hear the pain in her voice. 'I did want you to come here, to see him because he idolises you. He never forgave me for walking out on the marriage, just as he never forgave Alexio for leaving him without an heir.'

The mention of her brother brought a fresh wave of anger rushing over him. Alexio had been so threatened by him, so angry Kostas had a place in Sebastianos's heart as well as Athena's.

But had he ever really had a place in her heart?

He dismissed that traitorous question. They had loved with such passion he must have once. There just wasn't any room now.

'Everything you'd ever said – or did – made me more and more convinced you wanted to take Alexio's place in not just Father's affections, but his business.' She frowned in confusion then continued. 'For years you were always there, always in the background.'

Did she have any idea it was because of her he'd always been there? Not for any ill-gotten desire to take anything away from her or Alexio.

Kostas shook his head, seeing the pain that truth had cost her. 'No, Athena, I never wanted that.'

He'd had to stand back and watch her for years. Even before she went away to university, she'd been battling for recognition. He could see that clearly now, just as he could see how it all looked to her now.

'But...' She interrupted him, leaning forward.

Kostas continued. 'I wanted to help you.' He paused, a smile sliding into place. 'But I know how fiercely independent you are.'

'Kostas...' She paused, as if she wanted to add something else, but thought better of it.

He needed to think, needed time to process his feelings, the way she'd unlocked his heart when he'd lowered his guard. He loved her. He wanted her to remain his wife, but she was making it clear this was still nothing more than a deal.

Because he loved her, he wanted her to be happy. He

didn't want her to live in fear of the day he'd demand his terms of their deal – even if until that day they could live and love as passionately as they had been doing in the last twenty-four hours.

'Our deal is off,' he said as he opened the door of the bedroom, turning to look at her. 'You've got what you wanted, what you deserve.'

'Where are you going? It's the early hours of the morning.' Trepidation filled her voice as he moved to leave the bedroom.

'To the guest room.' She frowned at his response.

'After what just happened? Why?'

'Because of what just happened, Athena.'

She lifted her feet onto the chair, hugging her legs to her, as if she were trying to curl up and hide from the truth. He'd give her a little longer, then tomorrow they'd both had to face the truth – whatever that was.

Athena watched Kostas as he left the room, her heart heavy with sadness. She loved him but couldn't tell him, not after his stern silence when she'd cried out her love as she'd been transported to that wonderful place of oblivion he'd always taken her to as they'd made love.

But he hadn't made love, she reminded herself again.

She reached for the wooden case containing the Stefana crowns she and Kostas had worn on their wedding day. As she opened the case and took out the white intricate crowns joined by a white ribbon, her heart felt like it was ripping in two.

She'd been so happy that day and as the crowns were changed between them, crossing over in a tradition so old, she'd thought she'd never be torn apart from the man she loved.

When he'd fought her corner at the hospital, proving he'd be there for her, she'd known she'd never stopped loving him but had been too afraid to analyse that realisation. Let alone admit it. That moment had unlocked the doors of the past, brought everything out as well as beginning to smash down her barriers, and making love tonight had demolished them completely.

She loved Kostas. And he wanted to walk away.

Holding a crown in each hand, she got up and went to the doorway of the bedroom, pausing to stand in the doorway when she saw Kostas looking out of the floor-to-ceiling windows of the sitting room, the soft light of the almost full moon shining in on him.

He was looking upwards, as if he was seeking answers to unasked questions, and her chest tightened, her love for him wrapping around her heart.

She looked down at the crowns in her hands and put them together into one hand. If only it was as simple as that for her and Kostas. Slowly she walked into the room, bathed in moonlight. Kostas was lost in thought, her bare feet silent as she moved closer to him, holding the crowns in the silk folds of her dressing gown.

'Kostas.' She whispered his name and he turned to look at her.

His expression was stern. Unforgiving. 'I will return to Crete first thing tomorrow.'

She shook her head. 'Why?'

He looked at her without saying a word. The silence as deafening as it had been when he hadn't responded to her cried out declaration of love. She bit her lip, hoping, praying, shouting inside her head into the silence.

'I meant what I said, Athena. I will not be demanding my terms are met.' He turned back to the window, back to the view of moonlit Athens.

'But I haven't ...' she stumbled over her words. 'Our deal? A baby?'

She swallowed as the words left her lips, relief flooding through her, chased harshly by the realisation that not demanding his terms were met, almost certainly entailed releasing her from their marriage.

'I am many things, but I am not cruel. I will not force you to do something you fear so badly.'

Athena's heart hammered. This was facing her biggest fear head on. Her instinct was to run. Just as she'd done nine months ago. Her mouth dried and she swallowed hard, desperate to moisten the parchedness. She wanted to tell him she loved him. And that if he loved her, she'd try and face her fear. Find a way to get over it, see past it to what she wanted and ultimately to give him what he wanted.

She cast her eyes down, absently playing with the ribbon on the crowns. Tension hung heavy in the dim light of the room and she was acutely aware of Kostas watching her. Waiting for her to say something.

Slowly she looked up. 'I'm sorry. I wish I'd been able to tell you.'

'The fears of the past are the hardest ones to conquer.' His voice held a softer note. One of sympathy and understanding.

A ragged sigh escaped her, and she wished she could see his face, read the expression. See if it matched the new softness in his voice. They both had fears from the past to conquer. Was it possible that they could each help the other do just that? Salvage their marriage? Their love?

'We should have talked about having a family before we married.' He spoke into the heavy silence. 'I assumed it was something you'd want. And for that I'm sorry.'

Athena took a deep breath. 'I want to conquer my fear.' She paused as her heart hammered even louder, hardly able to believe the words leaving her lips. But she meant it. She'd face anything for the man she loved. Even pregnancy and childbirth. 'For us. I want to do it for us.'

In the shadows she could see his head shaking firmly and knew his lips would be pressed into a firm line. 'No.'

'Do you know the worst thing about my fear?' The tension increased, her question lingering between them, but having asked it gave her renewed strength.

Kostas remained silent. As if he knew it was a rhetorical question, that she was working past her demons.

'I want to be a mother.' The pitch of her voice raised, the urge to cry, to give in to panic, surged through her. She closed her eyes. Took a deep breath. 'I want to be the mother of your child.'

'No.' This time the word came at her with such ferocity she drew in a sharp breath. Panic charged through her. Not because of her fear, but because she was losing him. Losing her fight for the man she loved.

'You said you would be there for me.' The words were almost a strangled cry as she battled to hold back the tears.

All he'd said when she'd poured her heart out to him came back to her as if he'd just said the words.

Cementing the shocking need to have his baby, to go through something so scary, so terrifying with the man she loved. Because she loved him. Because he would be there for her. Just as he'd been all along.

'No. I will not – cannot – put you through that.'

She blinked away a determined tear, placing one crown in her other hand, bringing them together in front of her as Kostas remained tall and rigid, staring out to the night sky. She looked down at the crowns. He was so adamant. So savagely against it. Should she just cut the ribbon, let him go, meet someone else and have the child he wanted?

As if he sensed her preoccupation, he turned, looking down at the crowns in her hand, held apart. Her breath all but stopped as she watched him. The shadows on his face, cast by the moonlight, making his expression severe.

Then he stepped towards her, the shadows changed, and she saw raw emotion on his face and something more. Something which gave her hope – and courage to tell him what she'd been trying to hide from since the moment they'd agreed the terms of their deal.

'You kept them.' He spoke quietly, coming towards her, and she could now see sadness in his eyes. Pain that matched hers. Her heart lurched with hope.

'Yes,' she whispered as her eyes held his. Couldn't he see her love for him in hers?

He reached out and took one of the crowns from her, linking them together with the white ribbon as they had been on their wedding day.

'I was so in love with you that day,' she said almost in a whisper, watching as he looked down at the white crown he held gently in one hand. 'It felt like we'd always be together – joined like this.'

With her free hand she touched the white ribbon and he looked at her, his eyes dark with regret and sadness. 'We can't be. It's not right.'

'But...' Her voice was a cracked whisper, further words failing her.

He shook his head and she saw his throat move as he swallowed down his emotions. Was he locking them away? Shutting her out? 'We can't be together, not like this. Not because of a deal.'

'Forget the deal.' Desperation made her words suddenly loud and he looked at her again.

'I release you from the deal – and our marriage.'

'No,' she breathed the word as despair filled her. 'I don't want to be released from the deal – or our marriage. I love you, Kostas.'

CHAPTER TWELVE

'I DON'T DESERVE your love, Athena,' he said gruffly, handing back the crown, severing the connection the ribbon had briefly made.

'Don't say that.' Her words implored him to listen, but he ignored them. How could he look into her eyes and see all that love – for him? She'd believed he wanted to take everything from her, or worse, force her into a situation that had made her face her deepest fear, yet she'd still loved him.

Damn it, he should be the one to support her, doing whatever it was she needed him to do. Instead he'd goaded her as she'd asked him to do just one thing for her. He'd stood beside his pool, angered at the lust firing through him, forcing her to accept his preposterous terms.

But he hadn't known of her past then. Since that startling revelation he'd researched the fear of pregnancy, finding it had a name. He knew now his beautiful wife was so traumatised by the night she'd seen her mother go into early labour that she was suffering from primary tokophobia. And that was only compounded by her belief that she was invisible to her father as anything other than his daughter and that the old man saw him as his heir.

Damn it. He'd threatened to take it all from her. What kind of monster was he?

Inside he growled like an angry lion. He hated the vow he'd made with Elias, even if it had been with good and honourable intentions. It was a vow that had made him selfish and so focused on what he wanted, that he'd never taken any notice of the warning signs. Not even in those early days of his marriage had he seen what he was doing to the woman he loved.

And there had been plenty. Her insistence she needed to work, to be active in the family business. Her reluctance to talk about children and the future. If he had only listened, even once, she might have talked, might have confided in him.

Then it hit him like a hurricane making landfall. And he had to know.

'Why did you leave me?'

She blinked rapidly as she looked at him, taken aback by the change of direction in the conversation. The silver moonlight caressed her face in a way he itched to do, making her look pale – scared.

'I believed Alexio,' she said but her voice trailed off, as if she knew he'd worked it out for himself.

He moved closer to her, his heart breaking for her and all he'd made her face. The fear and pain that had made her run from him, from his love.

'It wasn't anything he'd said, was it? That was just a cover.'

Her eyes widened and he saw her take a long slow breath in, then let it go with a sigh, her eyes closing as she bit her lower lip. When she opened them again, it was like looking into her soul, right to the very heart of her.

'I don't think I ever believed Alexio,' she said softly, so softly he almost didn't hear her. 'But it gave me a way out. I was scared. Terrified of losing everything. All I'd worked for. My identity. But worse, of having to face my fears or admit I couldn't give you what you wanted.'

'And I made you feel like that.' His voice was feral with exasperation. 'I made you feel the only option was to run.' He'd failed her. Let her down in the worst way possible.

Courage filled Athena and she reached for Kostas, but suddenly shy of his almost naked body, she drew back her hand, swallowing down the nerves. He knew. She'd finally been able to admit she had used Alexio's lies as an excuse.

'I did it to myself.'

'No.' Anger glinted in his eyes as she looked up at him quickly. With a suddenness that made her gasp, he took hold of her hands, locking them around the crown she held in each hand, locking them together in a way the ribbon had no hope of doing. 'None of this is your fault.'

'I left you because I didn't have the courage, not only to have children with you, but to lose everything to you. The man I loved. Believing you'd been unfaithful seemed easier.' Tears filled her eyes, but she blinked them away, not wanting them to fall. She couldn't be that weak.

He let one of her hands go and brushed his hand down her hair, the curls of last night now wild and unruly.

'Now I understand why.' The tenderness in his voice, his touch, made her heart break with love for him. 'I would have understood then too. Because I loved you.'

He'd loved her. Past tense. She closed her eyes against the pain, the knowledge that she'd destroyed everything they'd ever had.

'I left you because of a stupid fear.'

His voice hardened again. 'You left me because you hadn't faced the trauma of the night your mother died or the ramifications of losing Alexio. I should have guessed, should have put it all together myself and realised. It is a recognised condition.'

'It is?' Disbelief echoed in her whisper.

'Yes, my sweet Athena. It is.' Sympathy filled his voice, replacing the hardness of seconds ago.

She'd never dared investigate. Never dared tell anyone. Too scared to acknowledge she needed help. But all that was over now. The darkness of that fear was slipping away as fast the night once the dawn broke.

'Telling you has made me see how much it had a hold on me.' She smiled weakly at him, searching for a hint of the love he'd once had for her. Had she totally destroyed it? 'And I want to overcome it.'

'So brave.' His whisper was so soft, a shiver slipped down her spine. 'My beautiful, brave love.'

'I want to be brave, with you there to help me.' She looked down at the crowns, not realising how tightly she'd been holding them. Then she looked into his eyes. 'And with your love.'

Kostas felt the stab in his heart as if a knife had been driven through his back. Even now he was letting her down, forcing her to beg for his love. But it was more than that. She was prepared to overcome her biggest fear, a terror so bad she'd run from him, and give him what he'd wanted. A child of his own flesh and blood.

'You have my love, Athena, and because of that love, I will walk away – if you want me to.'

He felt like he was taking the biggest gamble ever. He'd made deals for everything from food when he was a young boy to prime building land as a man, but nothing had been as high stakes as this moment.

The moon slipped behind a cloud, casting them into almost darkness. He watched her face as it darkened until he couldn't see her expression.

The cloud cover moved, freeing the moon, and Athena's face lightened, but the tension was intense.

'Don't walk away, please.'

He closed his eyes in relief and heard her move. He stood there, unable to do anything, then her lips brushed over his so gently he wondered if he'd imagined it. He opened his eyes and looked directly into hers.

'Stay and love me.'

He crushed her against his body, her arms wrapping willingly around him as he kissed her, allowing all the love he felt to surge into her. Then he pulled back, needing to see her face.

'I do love you, Athena, so very much.'

She smiled at him and it was as if the sun had replaced the moon. As if choirs were singing the highest notes possible. 'I love you too, Kostas, and I want to have your baby.'

'No.' He shook his head slowly. 'No babies.'

'But you want an heir. What about everything you said to my father? The passion in your words was so intense.'

'That was whilst I was still being a damned fool.'

'I don't understand?'

'As a young man I made a vow, that I would marry the right woman and never do what my father did me and my mother. I wanted to be a better father than mine. I wanted love in my life. The only person who knew the full extent of this vow was Elias. And when he died, it drove me even harder.'

'I want you to keep it.' Her words were lighter, but that was only half the story.

'I also vowed to have children. Not just heirs of my flesh and blood to inherit the empire I intended to create, but children to create the loving family I'd never had.'

Saying it aloud seemed so silly, so childish, and so very selfish. Kostas felt shame burn through him.

'And you wanted that to honour Elias's memory?' Her expression was so intense, so full of pain as she looked at him.

He sighed heavily, ashamed of who he'd become. Convinced he was even more unworthy of her than he'd ever been. 'Trying to do that has made me unworthy of you, of your love.'

'No...' she began, but he pressed his finger to her lips,

silencing her denial.

'Let me finish, tell you the whole sorry story.'

He moved his finger from her lips and expectant silence slipped around them.

'I always felt unworthy of you and worked so hard to leave my past behind, but it's always there, waiting in the shadows.'

He cast a glance around the room, expecting to see images from his childhood come racing from the dark corners of the room.

'I've broken almost every law a man can break. My wild and reckless need to fight the world which turned its back on me, made me nothing. It took every last bit of self-respect from me, and your father gave me the chance to earn back that self-respect, bit by bit. But I have never been worthy of a woman like you, of your love.'

Athena listened to the heart-breaking story of his childhood, desperately wanting to hold him, to kiss away the doubt and fear. 'That is why you didn't come after me when I left, why you didn't fight for me – or us?'

He nodded silently and she knew they'd reached the point where there wasn't a single barrier between them. They were joined in a far more meaningful way than the white ribbon of the crowns had ever done.

'We need a new vow.'

He frowned at her, but still he said nothing.

'To never allow our past hurt, past experiences, to come between us and our love.'

Again, he closed his eyes but this time she didn't reach up and kiss him. She watched as the last tension slipped from his broad shoulders. Shoulders that would carry her through every month of pregnancy and to the motherhood she'd secretly longed for. It would be terrifying, but she'd have Kostas. And his love.

He sighed in relief, opening his eyes. 'I love you, Athena. You've freed me to be the man I could be. A better man than my father.'

She smiled. 'I love you, the man who is far more worthy of my love than he knows. The proud, successful man, born out of a childhood that could have made you so different. And you will make the most amazing father.'

'We can adopt, any child we bring up together will be ours. You will make a wonderful mother.'

She pressed her palm to his face. 'Saying that is the greatest gift you can ever give me. I love you, Kostas, so very much.'

Kostas kissed her softly and gently and she knew everything was right between them, that they could move forward – together.

'You are my life, Athena,' he whispered against her lips as the embers of their passion grew warmer by the second. 'And I want you by my side, as my wife, no matter what.'

EPILOGUE

Sixteen Months Later

ATHENA LOOKED into the cradle of baby Viki, their New Year blessing, now just weeks old. She smiled at the tiny baby and then looked up at Kostas, her heart overflowing with love – for both of them.

'I'm so proud of you,' Kostas said as he smiled at her, then looked down at his sleeping daughter. The baby that would inherit his empire.

'She is so beautiful.' Athena stroked her finger over the softness of Viki's cheek. She was so perfect. So adorable, and Athena couldn't imagine life without her. Or Kostas.

'Thank you,' she whispered as she looked into Kostas's eyes.

'What for?' Kostas said with a smile lifting his lips in that sexy way.

'For being there for me, every step of the way. For caring enough to do that. But most of all, for understanding...' She paused. 'For loving me despite everything, all the appointments and visits. And for putting up with me when my panic got the better of me. I've probably been hell to live with.'

Kostas looked down at the sleeping baby. 'Every minute, every dark moment, every jubilation over another milestone or goal reached, was worth it. For her. And for you, because I love you, Athena, so very much.'

'I couldn't have done it without you and even though I was terrified as she grew inside me, I trusted you to be there for me and our baby. And you were. All the way.'

A tear slipped from her eye as she smiled up at her husband, the man who'd helped her overcome her darkest fear and achieve her most secret desire. The man she loved with all her heart.

'I am always here for you,' he said, taking her in his arms.

'I love you so much, Kostas.'

He smiled at her. 'It's bad to say, but I wish your father wasn't visiting this afternoon. I'd like nothing more than some quiet time with you.'

Athena laughed softly. The happiness that her father's health had been regained, that he'd been able to meet his granddaughter, was always with her. 'I'm just thankful he's well again, that he fought not just for his life, but for me too. He's making up for lost time now, being the doting grandfather.'

'That's why I feel bad,' Kostas kissed her lightly on the nose. 'But I can't help the way you make me feel.'

'And why would that be?' she teased. 'Is it because we have much to celebrate? Like the merger between the Petrakis empire and Kyriakou Construction?'

Kostas shook his head. 'Always business with you.' His tone was light and teasing, but it had a serious undertone. He still often had to persuade Athena to allow others to take on her projects, to slow down and enjoy being a mum. Gradually she was, but this week was about much more than a business merger.

Something far more important.

It was about the new daughter lying in her crib and, in just a few weeks, celebrating two years of marriage.

'I'm sorry,' Athena laughed up at him, looking radiant. 'Forgive me?'

'I will always forgive you.' He pressed his lips to hers. 'But I was thinking more about us. Almost two years ago, we married.'

Athena grew serious. 'When I think how I nearly threw it all away.'

'That's my line,' he said, shaking his head. 'But none of that matters now. Your father's health is recovered, my vow to Elias is fulfilled and we have a beautiful baby girl and two years of marriage to celebrate.'

'In that case,' Athena teased again. 'I look forward to celebrating with you. I love you so much.'

Kostas lowered his lips to hers, holding her close, feeling her delicious body against his. 'I never thought I feel so complete, so much love.' A powerful emotion surged through Kostas and he knew he was and would always be a better man for having this woman in his life. 'You have made me so happy. I love you, Athena. So very much.'

The End

ACKNOWLEDGMENTS

To my readers, thank you for reading my books and for any readers who leave reviews, I am very grateful. It warms my heart to see that readers have enjoyed the stories I've enjoyed creating.

Thanks also to my editor, proof-reader and cover designer, and Fabrian Books for welcoming me into the family.

Thank you to all my writing friends and especially The Write Romantics, who have been there with advice and support long before my first book was published.

Lastly and by no means least, thank you to my family for their support and belief.

ABOUT THE AUTHOR

Rachael Thomas has been an avid romance reader for as long as she can remember and has dreamed of writing her own romance stories almost as long. With sixteen titles published by Harlequin/Mills and Boon since being in the top ten of Harlequin's So You Think You Can Write competition in 2013 this dream has certainly come true. Now she likes nothing more than to write romances set against the backdrop of glamorous international settings, a total contrast to her daily life on the family farm in Wales. This is her first title for Fabrian Books. Visit her at rachaelthomas.co.uk

ALSO BY RACHAEL THOMAS

Married For the Italian's Heir

The Sheikh's Last Mistress

From One Night to Wife

Di Marcello's Secret Son

Just some of the titles published by Harlequin and Mills and Boon.

Printed in Great Britain
by Amazon

57360138R00118